PRINCE OF DORKNESS

Mo̲r̲e̲ Notes from
a TOTALLY LAME VAMPIRE

BY Tim Collins

ILLUSTRATED BY Andrew Pinder

ALADDIN · New York   London   Toronto   Sydney

🪔 ALADDIN

An imprint of Simon & Schuster Children's Publishing Division

1230 Avenue of the Americas, New York, NY 10020

First Aladdin hardcover edition September 2011

Copyright © 2011 by Michael O'Mara Books Limited

Published by arrangement with Michael O'Mara Books Limited

Originally published in Great Britain in 2011 as Diary of a Wimpy Vampire: Prince of Dorkness by Michael O'Mara Books Limited

For information about special discounts for bulk purchases, please contact Simon & Schuster Special Sales at 1-866-506-1949 or business@simonandschuster.com.

The Simon & Schuster Speakers Bureau can bring authors to your live event. For more information or to book an event, contact the Simon & Schuster Speakers Bureau at 1-866-248-3049 or visit our website at www.simonspeakers.com.

Designed by Jessica Handelman

The text of this book was set in Carnes Handscript.

Manufactured in the United States of America 0811 FFG

10 9 8 7 6 5 4 3 2 1

Library of Congress Cataloging-in-Publication Data

Collins, Tim, 1975-

Prince of Dorkness : more notes from a totally lame vampire / by Tim Collins ; illustrated by Andrew Pinder. — 1st Aladdin ed.

p. cm.

Summary: After changing from lame to super-attractive over school break, vampire Nigel acquires a girlfriend, Chloe, and starts the new term as one of the most popular students at school, but then a new student sets his sights on Chloe, and Nigel must compete for her affections.

ISBN 978-1-4424-3388-5 (pob ed.)

[1. Vampires—Fiction. 2. Werewolves—Fiction. 3. Schools—Fiction. 4. Love—Fiction. 5. England—Fiction. 6. Diaries—Fiction.] I. Pinder, Andrew, ill. II. Title.

PZ7.C69725Pr 2011   [Fic]—dc23   2011012349

ISBN 978-1-4424-3389-2 (eBook)

ACKNOWLEDGMENTS

Thanks to Collette Collins, Lindsay Davies, Andrew Pinder, Toby Buchan, Kate Moore, Sarah Sandland, Ana McLaughlin, Jennifer Christie, Jane Graham Maw, Kiera Williamson, Jamil Bhatti, and Dan Coxon.

Thanks also to everyone at the Vampire Council for responding to my telegraphs so promptly.

—T. C.

WEDNESDAY, AUGUST 31

School starts again tomorrow. It will be the first time I've seen my true love Chloe in two weeks, as she's been on holiday with her parents in Greece. She invited me to go with them, but I was worried the sun would hurt my skin. Plus, I didn't want all those mosquitoes sucking my blood. Which is rather hypocritical, I know.

BLAGH!

1

THURSDAY, SEPTEMBER 1

Today I was reunited with Chloe, though I was disappointed to see she had a tan. It's not a look that does much for me, even if it's a genuine tan caused by sunshine rather than wood varnish or whatever our home economics teacher, Mrs. Molloy, uses. Still, a few days moping around with me should soon return Chloe's lovely long neck to its usual pale color.

Other than Chloe's tan, the only surprise today was a new pupil called Jason. He has a massive potato-like head and his eyebrows meet in the middle, so I expect he'll be

2

the new school bully. I'll probably have to protect all these humans from him with my vampire strength. Not that I'll get a word of thanks, but such is my responsibility as a superior being. It is my gift and my curse.

FRIDAY, SEPTEMBER 2

Today the principal gave us a serious talk about how we're starting sophomore year now, and we'll soon take the exams that will determine what we do for the rest of our lives.

Mine won't. Whether I get 100 percent or cover my paper with offensive cartoons of the exam supervisor, my fate will be the same. I'll have to move to another school in another town and start again as a freshman next September so nobody notices that I never get any older. And sometime before then, I'll have to decide whether to transform Chloe into a vampire or leave her behind forever. It's quite stressful, really. I don't want to think about it right now.

Chloe has clearly been thinking about it, because she mentioned transformation several times this summer. I changed the subject whenever she did, of course. She's known that vampires are real for only a few months, so she can't possibly know if she's ready to turn yet. Plus, I'll have to get Mum and Dad's permission, and that's going to cause a bigger headache than sniffing a large portion of garlic bread with an extra topping of garlic.

SATURDAY, SEPTEMBER 3

I went out to Stockfield Moor with Chloe today. I feel like we have a close bond since that day last month when she let me drink her blood.

That's right, I just thought I'd throw it in casually there. I'm finally a real, grown-up vampire now that I've drunk some actual human blood using my own fangs. I don't think it would be gentlemanly of me to describe it in detail, even in a secret diary, but let's just say that the experience was everything I'd hoped it would be.

I expect we'll do it again soon, but we'll have to wait for Chloe's parents to go away again so they don't barge in halfway through, causing me to pretend she fell over and pierced her neck on two thumbtacks that I was removing with my teeth.

We had an enjoyable walk on Stockfield Moor, and when no one was around, I showed Chloe my vampire strength by uprooting a tree. But she said it was bad for the environment, so I had to put it back in the ground again.

She said that we should care for the planet if we're both going to be around to see it. I could see she was trying to steer the conversation around to transformation again, but I didn't take the bait. I'd rather just enjoy our time together and forget about long-term commitments.

On the way home I picked up a Coke can and put it in a recycling bin to offset the damage I'd done by uprooting the tree.

SUNDAY, SEPTEMBER 4

I went downstairs to get a thermos of blood this morning,* and I heard my sister having a

---

*Yes, I still rely on Mum and Dad to drain blood from humans and leave it in the fridge for me. So what? While it's true that I could attack humans myself now that I've got my vampire strength and speed, Mum and Dad are more experienced at getting away with it, so I'm happy to let them carry on. Plus, I'm a pacifist, so it wouldn't be fair to make me carry out violent acts on strangers.

massive tantrum because Mum and Dad won't let her go to Pizza Hut for her friend's birthday party. She wanted to go along and drink blood from her Hannah Montana thermos, but they wouldn't let her.

You know what I think? Let her learn the hard way. Let her go ahead and spoil the party by guzzling blood in a horrifying fashion while all her friends are biting into their stuffed crusts. Then we'll see how many more parties she gets invited to.

MONDAY, SEPTEMBER 5

I'm pleased to report that my popularity hasn't worn off over the summer holidays. For the first time in my century on this planet, I'm cool in more than just the sense of body temperature.

Jacqui passed me this note in English class this morning:

Dear Nigel,
I think u r lush. Will u go out with me?

B.O.L.T.O.P. (Better On Lips Than On Paper)

Love,
Jacqui
P.S. Katie thinks u r fine 2, but she don't want me to rite it. LOL!

While Jacqui's rhetoric failed to move me, I was pleased she'd attempted a love letter, and I made a point of showing it to Chloe, to remind her she's going out with a heartthrob. I wasn't being arrogant; I just don't want her to take me for granted.

I've just had a rather uncomfortable thought. If I choose to transform Chloe, she'll also develop vampire beauty,* which will mean every boy in school will like her. I'm not sure how I'd feel about that. On the one hand, I'd be proud to have a girlfriend everyone thinks is attractive; but on the other hand, I might get jealous when boys flirt with her. If one of them handed her a romantic note,

---

*Vampires have evolved to appear beautiful to humans so they can attract them and harvest their blood in much the same way that cats have evolved to appear cute to humans so they don't have to bother catching their own food. They fall for it every time, those humans.

I might attack and kill him in a jealous rage before I knew what I was doing.

All in all, I think I'd rather Chloe didn't develop supernatural allure and have boys fawning over her all the time. I know this might seem old-fashioned, but I am over one hundred years old, so I think I can be permitted one or two outdated views.

Anyway, I'm pretty progressive as vampires

go. You should hear Dad after he's had a few pints of blood. He once told me that things were better in the days when male vampires were allowed up to seven brides! I'd like to hear him say that when Mum's around.

TUESDAY, SEPTEMBER 6

The new kid, Jason, sat next to me in English this morning. I tried to make conversation, but I couldn't find any common ground. When I asked him what his hobbies were, he said Manchester United and monster trucks. I tried to talk to him about *Pride and Prejudice*, which we are supposed to have read for English, but he said it was boring. He obviously isn't sensitive and romantic like me.

I didn't want to ostracize him, but I really couldn't be bothered trying anymore, so I turned away and chatted to Craig and Sanjay instead.

After the lesson I heard that Jacqui is now using a picture of me as the screen saver on her phone. I told Chloe, and I could tell she was getting jealous. I suppose it was vain of me to mention it, but you can hardly blame me. Until I developed supernatural attractiveness earlier this year, I was the world's only lame vampire. So you might have to forgive me for wallowing in the attention a little.

WEDNESDAY, SEPTEMBER 7

I don't have many positive things to say about Jason, but I have to admit he's good at soccer. He was on the other team today, and he showed some fairly impressive skills.

I'm under strict instructions from my parents not to use my supernatural speed and strength in PE class,* so I deliberately missed a couple of chances early on in the game. But when I saw how easily Jason was slotting goals away, I couldn't resist stepping things up a little.

I'm getting better at controlling my powers now. I can dash down the playing field without turning into an unsettling blur of motion, and I can kick a ball into a net without ripping it apart. I increased my speed as subtly as I could and soon our teams were tied. Then, just as I was about to score the winner, Jason tripped me up and I tumbled awkwardly to the ground. That would have really hurt if I could feel pain!

---

*Dad thinks everyone would chop our heads off or whack stakes through our hearts if they found out we were vampires. I'm not so sure. I think it's more likely that we'd be given a reality TV series and an invitation to a fan convention. But it doesn't really matter what I think. His coven, his rules, as he reminds me so often.

Luckily, the PE teacher saw it. I was awarded a free kick, and I was delighted to see Jason step up and form part of the wall. Choosing revenge over glory, I kicked the ball right at his potato head.

For a moment I wondered if I'd blasted the ball too hard and his head would be knocked right off his shoulders and into the top corner of the net. But the weird thing was, he absorbed the blow without flinching, and a couple of minutes later he even managed to score the winner for his own team. I think Jason might be what's known as a genuine "hard case."

THURSDAY, SEPTEMBER 8

Word of Jason's victory must have spread, because today I saw him sitting with the tough gang in the smokers' corner, which is the bit of the playground farthest away from the staff room window. He should be careful hanging around with that lot. They'll pressure him to do a dare like climbing on the science building's roof or throwing a firecracker down a toilet.

After school I went to the park with Chloe to show her the backflips I've been practicing. She said I should work them into a dance routine for the school talent night, which they've optimistically chosen to call "Stockfield Comprehensive's Got Talent." I'm tempted, but

I expect Dad would count this as an explicit display of my powers.

Chloe then grilled me about what it was like to unleash vampire strength, so I did my best to make it sound boring even though it's the best thing in the world ever. She gets a really dreamy look when she talks about that stuff now. I can tell she's fixating on what it's like to be a vampire. She's even started reading all those paranormal romance books that feature male models wearing false fangs on the covers. As if those preening himbos could catch some prey. They'd be far too worried about breaking a nail.

I hope Chloe shuts up about transformation soon. If she doesn't, it's going to become a real issue between us.

Jay and Baz from the tough gang were trying out a new "joke" today. It involved telling everyone that new scientific research has proved that if your hand is bigger than your face, it means you've got cancer. I wonder which respected source they discovered this in? *New Scientist*? *Scientific American*? *The Journal of the Royal Society*?

The victim inevitably holds their palm in front of their face to check if they've got cancer, and Jay slams it right into their nose. They can't even tell a teacher because, technically, they hit themselves.

Obviously, it didn't work on me, and Jay only hurt his own hand when he tried to shove mine.

But there were plenty of pupils walking around with lovely fresh blood gushing from their noses, and I got so thirsty, I had to drink my lunch thermos of type O- early.

3:00 p.m.

Chloe told Mr. Morris about Jay and Baz's practical joke this morning, and apparently, they're angry with her. What was she supposed to do? It's part of her duty as a class officer to report antisocial behavior.

I told her she's got nothing to fear from the tough gang now that I've got my vampire strength. If any of them have a problem with her, they can come and see me about it. And I shall unleash hell. Or, at the very least, give them a Chinese burn.

6:00 p.m.

I got told off for laughing at a Shakespeare comedy in English today. Mr. Byrne was reading a scene from *A Midsummer Night's Dream*, and it reminded me of an amusing film version starring Mickey Rooney that I saw in the thirties.

Mr. Byrne asked me what I thought was so funny and if I'd like to share it with the rest of the class. I said the play was making me laugh, but he thought I was being sarcastic and made me stand outside the classroom. I admit that being one hundred years old means I've got slightly more traditional tastes than most pupils, but it's still a bit rich to tell me off for laughing at a comedy.

SATURDAY, SEPTEMBER 10
12:00 p.m.

Our bell rang early this morning, and when I opened the door, there was an old man standing there who wanted to speak to Dad. I wasn't quite sure how to respond and spent a while trying to work out if he was a vampire slayer or a local politician, as I'm under strict instructions not to let in either.

Eventually, I gave up and fetched Dad, and after a few murmured exchanges, he asked the old man to join him in his study. The old man wouldn't enter until Dad had recited some weird formal words inviting him in. I wonder what's going on.

20

Dad and the old duffer are still in the study. I hope he isn't a con man trying to trick Dad out of his money. I once caught him e-mailing his bank account details to someone claiming to be a Nigerian prince. To be fair, he did owe money to a genuine Nigerian prince he knew in the eighteenth century, so it was an easy mistake to make.

SUNDAY, SEPTEMBER 11

I'm not happy about this. Not one bit.

Early this morning Dad came into my room and explained that the old man is also a vampire. Apparently, his name is Cecil and he managed to trace us through some Scottish vampires Dad knows.

Dad said that Cecil became a vampire in the

late nineteenth century, and after a great deal of discussion, Dad had accepted that he was the one who'd transformed him.

Dad said he wanted to behave more responsibly to vampires he'd turned,* and so he'd agreed to let the old man join our coven. Before I could object, he told me to bring the old man's cases inside while he explained it all to my sister. To keep things simple, they haven't told her that other vampires

*We had a bit of trouble earlier this year with a vampire Dad transformed and abandoned in his wilder days. He's probably still feeling guilty about this and wants to go out of his way to help the vampires he's created. Which is all well and good, as long as he doesn't neglect the most important vampire he's created—me!

exist yet, so she'll have a lot to take in. It's fine, she only cares about herself, so it won't be a big deal. As Dad was leaving, he casually added that I should refer to Cecil as "Grandpa."

Grandpa? Really? Do I get a say in this?

I hope so-called Grandpa will be fetching his own blood supplies rather than dipping into ours. I need all the blood I can drink at my age, and I barely get enough as it is.

MONDAY, SEPTEMBER 12
3:00 p.m.

I sat in the library with Chloe at lunch. It's quite a romantic place for us because it's where I seduced her and claimed her heart earlier this year (after a couple of false starts).

I got annoyed when I saw she was reading a vampire romance novel called *Touch of the*

Forbidden Prince, which is part of a series called Dark Temptations.

Dark Temptations? We're a race of vicious blood drinkers, not a selection of chocolates. Why she feels the need to indulge in that far-fetched nonsense when she's got the real thing right here, I have no idea.

She looked rather distracted, so I assumed she was worrying about the prospect of losing me one day. But when I asked what she was thinking, it turned out she was obsessing about becoming a vampire yet again. Give it a rest!

I told her she must never again mention the topic of transformation inside the school grounds. I said this was to protect my identity, but the truth is, I'm just bored to tears by the subject. It's not like I don't hear enough nonsense about coffins and eternity at home.

I went to the park with Chloe after school, as I wasn't in much of a hurry to return to our crowded house. We had a cuddle on a bench and I really wanted to drink her blood, but I couldn't in case someone walked past. Needless to say, I was really thirsty by the time I got home, so imagine my dismay when I saw there was no blood left in the fridge!

Tellingly, Grandpa was sitting next to an empty thermos, with a trickle of dried blood on his chin. Thanks for saving me some, you selfish oaf.

Out of interest, what am I supposed to do? I can't attack anyone here in town without revealing myself as a vampire, so it looks like I'm just going to have to wait until Mum and Dad fetch some new blood tomorrow. I told Dad that Grandpa should be allowed to access the blood in the fridge only after all the main family members have fed, but he said it wouldn't make Cecil feel very welcome if we introduced that rule. But how does he think I feel when I have to go thirsty all night?

In the meantime, I shall try to take my mind off my thirst by watching Don't Look in the Attic, a DVD that Craig from school has lent me.

2:00 a.m.

My movie plan didn't work very well. The film was really gory and featured explicit shots of blood spurting from severed limbs, so it was a bit like a human trying to stave off their appetite by watching a cooking show.

TUESDAY, SEPTEMBER 13

3:00 p.m.

Jason showed everyone his new iPhone in math this morning, and all the silly humans were fawning over it. It didn't impress me. I've got so used to new technology coming and going that these trivial gadgets no longer excite me. It seems like only a moment ago that a boy named Brian Palmer brought a Walkman into school, and you'd have thought he had a working time machine from the excitement it caused.

I don't understand why Jason even needs a phone. It's not like he's got anything intelligent to say. He looks like he should communicate through smoke signals rather than text messages.

7:00 p.m.

Craig was reading a book about horror in English today, and he said that my mum looked like the Bride of Frankenstein. I thought he was disrespecting my family, so I went over to give him a dead arm, but when he showed me the picture, I had to admit it did look a bit like Mum. It wasn't much of an insult, really. If anything, she was out of the monster's league.

When I got home, I found that Mum and Dad had harvested some lovely thermoses of type AB+. It was very sweet and obviously taken from someone with high blood-sugar levels. Whomever it came from should probably go see a doctor if they recover.

To make sure I don't miss out on my share of this lovely claret tomorrow, I've written my name on one of the thermoses in permanent marker.

I'm feeling much stronger after my blood feast, which is just as well, as I fully intend to dish out a humiliating defeat to Jason in PE tomorrow to make up for his disgraceful behavior last week.

11:00 p.m.

I just asked Dad if he'd buy me an iPhone, and he said no. He said he couldn't understand what was so good about them, which is hardly surprising, as he doesn't understand what's good about any mobile phones. He still thinks they're called "radiotelephones" for a start.

It's completely unacceptable. He lets smelly old men help themselves to our blood, yet when it comes to buying his only son a decent phone, he's not interested. It's not like he hasn't got the money. He's got loads stashed around the house, and he's been hoarding some of it for so long, it's become obsolete. Perhaps I should take a bag of gold doubloons down to Phones 4u and see if they'll swap them for an iPhone with a twelve-month contract.

WEDNESDAY, SEPTEMBER 14
1:00 p.m.

I just got told off by Mr. Morris for kissing Chloe. He said that it was against school rules and that if he caught us again, we'd both be in detention.

If being in love is a crime, then lock me up and

throw away the key. I'd be able to escape using my vampire strength, so it wouldn't be much of a punishment, but that's not the point.

I'm off to PE now. I like to get changed before everyone else so they don't see how pale my skin is. Also, we're playing badminton this afternoon and I want to make sure I get Jason as my partner. I know he's got brute strength, but I doubt he'll be any good at a sport that requires skill and dexterity.

8:00 p.m.

I turned up in the locker room ten minutes early, only to find that Jason was already there. I'm not surprised he also wanted to get changed early. His back is so hairy, I thought for a minute that I'd wandered into the Neanderthal wing of the Natural History Museum by mistake. He

wouldn't have to bother wearing a shirt at all
if it didn't look so repulsive.

   I managed to team up with him for badminton,
but sadly, he was pretty good at that, too. I was
planning to hold my powers back and let a few
shots hit the net, but he was playing so well that
I couldn't bring myself to do so. Plus, everyone

else was focusing on their own games, so I didn't think it would matter if I went for it.

It turned out that neither of us missed the shuttlecock at all, and we made a single rally last the entire class. It was only when Mr. Moss blew the whistle and told us to pack up that it became apparent that one of us would have to lose on purpose. I saw determination in Jason's eyes, and it was clear that he would rather play all night than miss a shot, so I held my racket up and let the shuttlecock fly past to show him he hadn't really beaten me. That didn't stop him from holding his arms in the air and whooping in a ludicrous manner, of course.

Fine, have your little moment in the sun. I don't care. I'm happy to let you shallow little humans have your victories. At the end of the day I'm the one who gets to live forever and bite the necks of hot girls, so I'm the real winner, whatever happens in PE.

THURSDAY, SEPTEMBER 15
11:00 a.m.

There's a bug going round school and almost everyone is out sick. I notice that the tough gang have all taken ill at the same time. Last time that happened, they were spotted dropping Cheez-Its on the heads of bald men from the balcony of the shopping mall. Jason seems fine, though. I expect viruses are so repulsed by the hair on his back that they stay well away.

Obviously, as a vampire, I'm immune to disease because of my healing powers. I could play hooky if I wanted, but when you've been up all night unlocking all the tracks on Gran Turismo, you rather welcome the change of environment.

6:00 p.m.

Despite my warnings about getting hooked on such rubbish, Chloe has now moved on to the second book in the Dark Temptations series, which is called *Lure of the Deadly Immortal*. Perhaps this is why she brought up the topic of transformation again as we walked home this afternoon.

When I told Dad I had a human girlfriend back in May, he gave me an ancient leaflet warning she'd get obsessed with the idea of transformation. At the time I thought it was just prejudiced old nonsense, but now I see it was true. Oh, weak human race! Why can't you enjoy the privilege of consorting with our kind without lusting after our shadowy domain?

Chloe kept pushing me for technical details of how I'd go about transforming her, so I gave in and explained. I said I'd have to drink her blood again, but this time I'd have to keep on going much longer and then cut open one of my veins and let my blood flow into hers until it revived her. Then, after a couple of days in bed, she'd be a blood-drinking immortal and never have to bother with her weekly groceries again.

I immediately began to regret using us as the

example in this hypothetical scenario, because she replied, "Yes! Let's do it, Nigel! I want to turn into a vampire!"

I have to say I was shocked by her audacity. I knew this request would come eventually, but I had no idea it would be so soon or so brazen. I mumbled something about how transformation is a big step and you should wait a long time before making the commitment, then pretended I had some important homework to do and darted off home.

I really don't know what to do now. I suppose I should talk to Dad, but I'm afraid he'll forbid me from ever seeing Chloe again.

FRIDAY, SEPTEMBER 16
6:00 p.m.
In English this morning Mr. Byrne told us we had to choose a novel to talk about next week.

One of the books on the list was Dracula, and I realized that I hadn't read it for eight decades, so I thought I'd give it a go. Better keep my copy hidden from Chloe, though. She'll only use it as another excuse to go on about transformation.

This afternoon we had an art lesson where we were supposed to paint bowls of fruit. Jason ignored these instructions and drew a dead body with loads of blood coming out of it instead. Everyone thought it was really cool and daring, but I didn't think much of his art skills. I tried to do a gory painting of my own, but it was so good, I made myself thirsty and had to sneak into the supply closet to drink some blood from my thermos.

I was really thirsty again by the time I got home, so I was dismayed to see Grandpa chugging from the thermos with my name on it! Can the old fool even read? I had to make do with the clotted dregs, which were hardly sufficient. When he left the room, I asked Mum why Grandpa can't harvest his own blood, and she said that it's hard for him to go out and hunt because he's old and frail.

He doesn't look very frail to me. The other day I saw him lift up a huge metal filing cabinet in Dad's study with just one hand because his bus pass had fallen underneath it.

11:00 p.m.

Chloe came round to visit this evening. She finds it too cold here because we never have the heat on, and Dad goes mental if anyone messes with the thermostat. I would use this as an excuse for a cuddle, but Mum has now introduced a

stupid rule where we have to keep the door to my room open whenever Chloe's over. It's because she thinks I'll be drinking Chloe's blood all the time, which isn't even true. If I wanted to drink her blood, I'd do it in her house when her parents are away. I wouldn't do it here with my immature sister barging in and destroying the mood. She even burst in and did a crude blood-drinking mime on her Tenderheart Care Bear today, and I had to get Mum to tell her to stop.

SATURDAY, SEPTEMBER 17

When I was down at the shopping mall today, I spotted Jason with his family. Let's just say it's not hard to see where he gets his looks from! He was with his mum, dad, and little sister, and they were looking through the shoes in the bargain bin outside JJB Sports like troglodytes inspecting rocks.

Everyone in Jason's family is tall and stocky like him, and they all have the same bushy eyebrows, even his mum and sister. I was really hoping Jason would buy some clearance sneakers so I could mock him in PE. Darren from school once bought a pair of sneakers with just two stripes on them and tried to add a third stripe with a Sharpie to make them look like Adidas, but it fooled no one.

Jason and his family soon gave up on the cheap shoes and sat down on a bench. Then, rather than going to Starbucks and getting coffees, Jason's dad went into the supermarket and bought them each a tin of corned beef, and they scooped the meat out with their fingers.

It was so disgusting. I know I always find the sight of humans feeding pretty rank, but I bet the sight of Jason and his family wolfing down bargain meat would have looked gruesome to even the scuzziest human.

SUNDAY, SEPTEMBER 18

Today my sister embarrassed us all by asking Dad where vampires come from. Although she's been a vampire as long as I have, she was only ten human years old when she turned, so she's too young to be told the facts of death.

My parents usually try to brush aside such questions by saying that when a mummy and a daddy vampire love each other very much, a bat delivers a vampire child, but this time Grandpa stepped in.

He said that great and powerful gods once

ruled over the earth, and humans worshipped them and made sacrifices to them. One of these gods wanted to meet his subjects, so he decided to become human for a day. However, he fell in love with a woman and chose to stay in human form so he could be with her. He let some of his spirit pass into her body and, in doing so, created a race that had the strength and beauty of the gods but could pass as human, and this race became known as "vampires." To this day, the spirit of the old god enters those selected as worthy to join the race. This supposedly explains why we still need the sacrifice of human blood to survive and why the symbols of newer religions like Christianity cause us distress.

Obviously, I'm old enough to know this is just a myth invented to cover up the gory truth, but I have to say I found Grandpa's speech compelling. It certainly did the trick with my sister, who said she felt proud to have been chosen by the ancient spirit, and I'm sure I saw Mum wiping a tear out of the corner of her eye.

MONDAY, SEPTEMBER 19
12:00 p.m.

I was late for school this morning because I had to wait for Grandpa to finish in the bathroom. While I'm sure he has to look his best for a day of lounging around and stealing blood supplies, some of us have actually got lives to be getting on with. I told him to leave the bathroom free between 7:30 a.m. and 8:30 a.m. in future, to give me enough time to floss my teeth, but he took no notice.

When you're late for school, you're supposed to write an excuse on a form and give it to a

46

teacher. I couldn't bring myself to write "Old man who's pretending to be my grandparent hogged the bathroom so I couldn't floss my fangs," so I wrote "Bus delayed" instead. Not that it stopped me from getting detention.

6:00 p.m.

The battery on Jason's phone ran out today, so he couldn't use it as a calculator in math. I offered to lend him mine, which can draw graphs and has loads of extra buttons you don't need until SATs. You should have seen his face! He looked like he didn't know whether to use it to add up the angles of a triangle or fashion it into a primitive spear. Maybe I should try to find him an abacus next time.

I'm sure Jason's only in the same group as me for math because he's new. As soon as he has to take a test, Mr. Wilson will realize he's stupid and put him down to the bottom class, and I won't have to listen to him adding up.

11:00 p.m.
I started *Dracula* this evening. I have to say I'm enjoying reading it again, although the language and technology seem much more old-fashioned now. Count Dracula himself is a very cool character and seems to be having

a wonderful time. I wish I could live in a decay-ing castle with loads of sexy vampire chicks at my beck and call! If any real vampire acted as irresponsibly as him, they'd get a stake through their frilly shirt in minutes.

Later on, my sister started playing her awful teen pop really loudly, which ruined the novel's spooky Victorian atmosphere, so I grabbed a thermos of blood and came down here to the graveyard to read.

I find graveyards at night very peaceful places. I suppose it must be part of my culture. At any rate, I'm having a relaxing time away from the stress of noisy families and high-maintenance girlfriends.

3:00 a.m.

This Van Helsing guy is an idiot.

49

TUESDAY, SEPTEMBER 20

Today I took Chloe's advice and signed up for the school talent contest so I can showcase my amazing backflips. I know I'm sort of breaking Dad's rules about displaying vampire powers, but last year I saw a boy on a TV talent show doing backflips as part of his act and nobody walloped a stake in him.

I have chosen to perform to a track called "I Like to Move It" by Reel 2 Real featuring the Mad Stuntman, and I spent tonight timing my jumps to it. I looked pretty cool (if I do say so myself) and I'm sure to win. At any rate, I'm bound to be better than Jason, who's signed up

to give a display of soccer skills, which I'm sure will be utterly fascinating to anyone with an IQ of single digits.

I had the misfortune to witness Jason eating his lunch today. Rejecting such popular staples as chips and sandwiches, Jason was content with a single can of Spam, which he gulped straight from the can. It was quite simply the most disgusting attempt at feeding I've ever seen. And this is coming from someone who's seen his sister trying to drink a glass of type A- when she had hiccups.

WEDNESDAY, SEPTEMBER 21
12:00 p.m.

I don't have a normal PE class this afternoon because I've signed up for the cross-country running club. Every Wednesday between now and Christmas, Mr. Moss will drive a group of us out to Pottsworth Moor and we'll run a circular course around it.

I was intrigued to see that Jason has also signed up for the club. He might have done well at soccer and badminton, but I can't see him excelling at an endurance sport. Not that he'd have any chance of beating me even if he were the world's greatest marathon runner. I could run ten times faster than any human if I wanted to. If I went to maximum speed, I'd open up a wormhole in the space-time continuum and everyone would be eaten by dinosaurs or something.

6:00 p.m.

I have to admit that Jason is pretty good at running, too. As we set off, I ran just fast enough to break away on my own but not so fast that I looked weird. Then when the path turned a corner

and I was out of sight, I was finally able to let loose. I ran right to the top of Pottsworth Moor and slid down on my back, relieved to drop the pretense of boring humanity.

After I'd got that out of my system, I dashed back to the course and adopted a more realistic pace again. I was surprised to see Jason emerging around the side of the hill behind me. I hadn't expected any of the other kids to catch up for at least another ten minutes. Even more surprisingly, he seemed to be gaining on me. By the time we had turned the last bend on the way back to the van, we both must have been bombing along at ten miles an hour. Mr. Moss looked surprised to see us returning so soon and quickly shoved his magazine into his bag.

In the end I had to let Jason inch ahead of me and complete the course first because I was worried about running too fast in front of Mr. Moss. It's fine—it's only cross-country running. It's not a race. Plus, next week I won't waste any time running up the hill; I'll just zoom round the course, finish first, and casually lean against the van waiting for Jason. I can't wait.

THURSDAY, SEPTEMBER 22
12:00 p.m.

Grandpa hogged the bathroom again until eight thirty this morning and made me late, so Mum had to give me a lift to school. She looked offended when I asked her to drop me off round the corner so no one could see us.

I explained that last time she dropped me off in front of everyone, all the boys said they fancied her. She said she was glad her supernatural beauty was still working. Then she asked why it didn't make me proud that all the little boys in my school liked her. Because it's embarrassing, that's why! It's fine to have a cell phone, a pair of sneakers, or even a girlfriend that other boys covet, but not a mum!

5:00 p.m.

I sat next to Jacqui in math today to see if she's still using my picture as her screen saver, and I was horrified to see that she's replaced it with one of Jason. At least, I think it was Jason. It

55

might have been Mr. Potato Head, I suppose.

Even worse, she spent all lesson asking me if I could introduce her to him. She'd heard all about his sporting prowess but made no mention of my own achievements.

What exactly does she see in him? Could he write moving poetry for her? Could he take her on romantic moonlit walks? I hope she likes watching soccer and eating canned meat, because that's about as far as her cultural life will extend if she ends up with that jerk.

2:00 a.m.

Tonight I've been playing the driving game I got from Games Exchange, but I'm already bored with it. I tire of games much more easily now. Perhaps it's because they don't offer me sufficient emotional depth now that I'm mature and have a girlfriend. Perhaps I no longer need escapism now that I'm living an exciting supernatural lifestyle. Or perhaps my fingers can move so fast now that I've got vampire speed that I can complete them too easily.

Whatever the reason, I've unlocked all the cars, won all the medals, and even whupped some kid in Tokyo through the online play mode, so it looks like I've got no excuse to avoid my homework. At least it involves reading about a sexy vampire. That's got to be more interesting than trigonometry.

FRIDAY, SEPTEMBER 23
7:00 a.m.

I was just finishing *Dracula* when Dad saw me and started going on about how Bram Stoker based the character on him. I think Dad is flattering himself, but I let him enjoy his delusion.

However, when I told him I was doing a talk about it in English, he got really angry and said I'd give away our identities. Who does he think my classmates are? Buffy, Blade, and the Frog brothers?

6:00 p.m.

I think my *Dracula* talk went well. I said it was a gripping read even though it was written over one hundred years ago, and Mr. Byrne was impressed that I'd chosen such an old book.

I stole quite a lot of my talk from the CliffsNotes study guide, which I know was lazy when I could have drawn on my own experience, but at least I bothered to read the book. When Craig spoke about *Lord of the Flies*, he just read the review quotes off the back. He probably would have got away with it if he hadn't read out the names of the newspapers they came from as well.

For the finale of my talk, I tried to engage the class by showing a clip of the 1931 film of *Dracula* on Mr. Byrne's computer. I shouldn't have bothered. Instead of cowering in fear as Bela Lugosi descended a crumbling staircase and introduced himself, they all burst out laughing!

I'll be the first to admit that the film doesn't stand up to today's 3-D blockbusters, but they ought to have shown a bit more respect for the serious subject matter. They wouldn't find it so hilarious if Mum and Dad pounced on them on their way home tonight.

After I'd finished, it was Jason's turn, and he did his talk about *Animal Farm*. At first I thought he was joking when he said it was an enjoyable story about horses and pigs, but it turned out that he'd read the entire book without understanding it was really about politics. Like, duh! Hello? Earth to Jason? This is the moment everyone in the class should have been laughing, but instead, they listened in silence. They probably couldn't understand what he was grunting about.

SATURDAY, SEPTEMBER 24
10:00 a.m.

It's Chloe's birthday on Tuesday, so I asked Dad for some money to buy her a present, and he gave me ten pounds. I tried to explain that this was hardly enough to declare eternal love, but he said it's the thought that counts. Yes, but only if the thought is, "I'm going to spend lots of money on you." I'll have to think of a way to turn this pittance into a larger amount using my vampire skills.

12:00 p.m.

Making money with my vampire powers was harder than I expected. Obviously, I could have used my vampire strength to mug people or my vampire speed to pick their pockets, but I've got too much of a conscience to consider any-thing of the sort.

At first I changed the bill into coins and tried to win money on the coin waterfalls in the amusement arcade. I used my strength to hurl the coins into the slot, expecting to create an avalanche of silver and a bumper payout. When this didn't happen, I began to suspect that the coins overhanging the bottom were glued in place. A firm shove of the machine confirmed my suspicion but set an alarm off and got me thrown out of the arcade.

Next, I tried the pub quiz machine in the Black Lion. I've sometimes heard people complaining that they'd have won money if the questions didn't come up so fast. I thought this would be a snap with my supernatural speed, but I forgot that I don't have a supernatural memory of FA Cup finals to go with it. I could have sworn it was Arsenal in 2001, not Liverpool.

On my way home I saw Jay and Baz from the tough gang. They were playing a game where you have to throw coins against a wall, and the person who gets one to land nearest the wall wins all the money. I had a go, figuring that if I lobbed my coin really hard at the wall, it would lodge in and I'd be unbeatable. Unfortunately, I threw the coin so hard, it ricocheted and smashed the window of a car. Jay said that under a special rule of the game he'd won my money and anything of value in the car's glove compartment.

So my efforts to make money have left me with a total budget of £3.60. I'm not sure how I'm supposed to declare my immortal love with that.

12:30 p.m.

It looks like my declaration of eternal love is back on again. Grandpa has asked me to help him carry some wood back from the store so he can make a coffin. I told him it would cost a hundred pounds, and he willingly handed it over from a huge wad of notes in his cape pocket. He clearly has no idea how much modern money is worth. I should have asked for a thousand.

7:00 p.m.

It was weird being out with Grandpa. I couldn't believe how much attention he got from older women. Some of them smiled flirtatiously, some of them blew kisses, and one of them even pressed a piece of paper into his hand with her phone number on it. I understand that all vampires need hypnotic beauty to attract victims, but I'm surprised the principle still holds for vampires who transform so late in life. He certainly doesn't look hypnotically beautiful to me.

Looking at all those wrinklies fawning over Grandpa made me glad I transformed when I did. Perhaps if I'd stayed human longer, I'd be able to appreciate older women more, but the idea of drinking from their prominent blue veins makes my fangs shrink right up.

Anyway, we carried the wood home (I was taking nearly all the weight, but I could hardly complain for the money I was getting), constructed the coffin, and covered the bottom with soil so it was comfortable to lie down in.

Of course, vampires don't really need to sleep in coffins because they don't sleep at all, but Grandpa insists on resting in a coffin every so often for the sake of tradition. And I'm going to hazard a guess that these periods of rest will occur whenever there's something to be done around the house.

SUNDAY, SEPTEMBER 25

I went round to Chloe's house today, and to be perfectly honest, my hopes were high that another session of drinking her lovely type O-blood was in the cards. Her parents were away visiting relatives, so it seemed like the perfect opportunity.

Chloe opened the door and bid me welcome into the shadowy realm of darkness, adding that I should take my shoes off first because her mum was neurotic about the new beige carpet.

All day she kept lapsing into nonsense about how she wanted to float away on a dark lake of eternity or some such thing. I wish someone would ban those silly books she reads. They make humans think that being a vampire is all brooding and pouting. They leave out all the tedious bits, like when you get on the circular night bus just to pass the time because you don't sleep.

I didn't know how to deal with Chloe's flowery requests for transformation, so I asked her what she thought we should do. She said that I should turn her right away so there wouldn't be too much of an age gap between us, and then she pulled her collar back to bare her neck!

Instantly, my thirst for blood gave way to my fear of commitment, and my fangs retracted. I found myself reeling off the kind of nonsense Dad usually comes out with. I asked her if she realized that she could never see her family again and if she truly understood what eternity would be like. It lasts a really long time, you know. Even longer than that double math lesson when Mr. Wilson went off-topic and talked about his motorbike for two hours.

Chloe looked deflated when I'd finished my rant and covered her neck up, so I said I really wanted to transform her but I'd need permission from Mum and Dad. I said I'd do my level best to get it, and she perked up.

MONDAY, SEPTEMBER 26
1:00 p.m.

Chloe was waiting for me outside the school gates this morning to let me know she hasn't changed her mind. I pretended I'd given Dad an impassioned speech about transforming her and I was awaiting his reply.

In truth, I'm dreading talking to Dad about it. He warned me this would happen as soon as I started going out with a human, and I'll never hear the last of it if I tell him he was right.

Plus, I'm not really convinced about Chloe's

motives for wanting to become a vampire. At lunch she started going on about how jealous her cousin will be when she transforms. I took this as evidence that she still doesn't understand what she's getting into. For a start, she won't be allowed to tell any humans if she joins our coven, so her cousin will never know. More to the point, once she realizes she has the rest of weary eternity stretching before her, she'll care little for such petty human rivalries. She might find she's the envious one by the time her cousin's funeral comes around.

10:00 p.m.

I went to the Goth shop tonight to choose Chloe's present. None of the gifts were really screaming eternal love at me, so I hedged my bets and bought her some scented candles, a mug in the shape of a skull, a dragon pendant, a coffin purse, a pumpkin thermos, and some spider earrings. Then, on the way home, I stopped off at the grocery store and bought a box of Sugar Puffs and a carton of orange juice. I'm not really sure why I bought those now. I think I just panicked.

Anyway, I piled it all together and wrapped it, and it looked like the kind of thing humans like.

TUESDAY, SEPTEMBER 27

Mum and Dad brought some lovely type O- back home this morning, so I made a point of pouring it into my thermos and telling everyone they shouldn't drink from it, so we wouldn't catch each other's germs. Dad said that if I'd seen the state of the tramp they'd drained it from, their germs would be the least of my worries. They all seemed to think this was hilarious, but I thought it was in poor taste, and I almost lost my appetite.

When I got to school, I gave Chloe her presents and a birthday kiss. She seemed pleased enough with the stuff I bought her, though she couldn't fit it all in her bag, so I had to keep the Sugar Puffs.

Then she said that there was one more birthday present I could give her, and I wondered if I should have bought the skeleton bank, too. It turned out she was going on about transformation again, yawn yawn.

She said it would be really romantic if we

sneaked out to the countryside so I could transform her today. That way her transformation day would be the same as her human birthday, and it would be easier to remember.

I told her that transformation requires careful planning and preparation, so we couldn't rush it. It doesn't, of course. Dad attacked Mum in a Paris graveyard two hundred years ago and had every intention of draining her and abandoning her. But he decided she was too good to waste on a light snack, so he took her back to his lair, and within a few days, she'd agreed to become his vampire bride. It's amazing their marriage has lasted when you think about the reckless way it began.

In the evening Chloe went out for a meal with her parents, so I went to Stockfield Moor to practice my performance for the school talent night. I tried to time my backflips with the music on my iPod, but my headphones kept falling off, so I gave up and jumped around randomly instead. It wasn't very good preparation, but it certainly helped to take my mind off my personal issues for a while.

WEDNESDAY, SEPTEMBER 28
8:00 p.m.

I was looking forward to beating Jason at cross-country running today, and I was getting ready to dial my powers up and thrash him. Sadly, I didn't get the chance, because he was out sick. I completed the course ages before anyone else, but it wasn't a satisfying victory without him there.

I expect he's got the illness that's going round, because that's the kind of pathetic thing humans do. So I didn't get a chance to humiliate him at running, but the fact remains that he got ill and I didn't, so I won the healthiness competition.

When I got home, I wanted to talk to Mum and Dad about Chloe, but they were listening to Grandpa drone on about all the powerful vampires he's known in the past, so I didn't get a chance. Grandpa was describing special vampire powers like telepathy, telekinesis, and precognition to my sister, and you can bet she was getting ideas above her station.

11:00 p.m.

Chloe is still coming on way too strong with the whole transformation thing. She just sent me a picture of her face with fangs Photoshopped on. I texted her back to say that it was a cool photo, but Dad would go mad if he saw it so she should delete it from her computer and phone. She agreed but signed off with V^^^^V, which is the emoticon vampire fans use instead of things like ;) and :(.

THURSDAY, SEPTEMBER 29
6:00 p.m.
This is getting out of hand now. On the way home from school Chloe asked if I'd be able to

bring her back to life as a vampire if she died in an accident. In truth, I could if I reached her soon enough. There are plenty of records of humans who were transformed because they'd just been killed and their vampire lovers didn't want to lose them. I was going to explain this to Chloe, but I thought she might throw herself under the number 73 bus, so I said it was unlikely.

It's all gone too far now. I'm going to tell Mum and Dad about it, and I'm going to do it right now.

12:00 a.m.

Well, I've told them now. As expected, Dad had a whale of a time reminding me that he'd warned me. I tried not to get angry, but I found his smug lecturing hard to take when you consider how he transformed Mum. I shouted,

"At least I didn't jump on her in a graveyard like a common ghoul!" and then I ran upstairs.

I still had my head under my pillow when Mum came upstairs with a mug of hot B+. She told me that I'd upset Dad with my comment and that he'd made mistakes in the past but he was a different vampire now, and his decision to let Grandpa stay proved that.

I was expecting her to forbid me from transforming Chloe at all, but instead, she asked me what I thought I should do.

At first I said that I should transform her right away because that's what she's asked for, but after talking it over, I admitted that more time was needed. It's not that I'm unsure about spending eternity with her, I just want her to understand fully what she's getting into. After all, it was only a few months ago that she had her heart set on taking a year off before college to help unfortunate people. Now she wants to drink their blood.

Mum suggested that I let Chloe think it over until the end of the year and then change her if she still wants to. After all, eternity is surely serious enough to spend three months waiting for. I agreed and told her to pass on my apologies to Dad for my outburst.

FRIDAY, SEPTEMBER 30
11:00 p.m.

This morning I told Chloe about my discussion with Mum and Dad. In my version of events,

I protested strongly against their strict rules, but they threatened me with expulsion from the coven if I didn't observe them.

Chloe said she understood, but I could tell she was disappointed. It's strange how the lure of immortality grips mortals and makes all their other ambitions seem trivial and pointless. She doesn't even want to become class president anymore.

I went out to Pottsworth Moor tonight to practice my backflips for the talent show, but I couldn't focus because I was worrying about Chloe so much. At one point my concentration lapsed so much that I let a huge brown dog, which I hadn't seen approaching, brush past me. I need to be more careful about avoiding animals, as they hate all vampires, especially me. Dogs, cats, squirrels, hamsters, gerbils, cows, wolves, sheep—all would ram a stake into my heart if they could lift one.

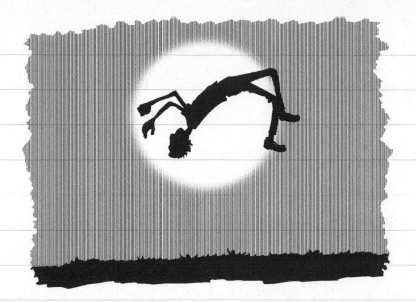

2:00 a.m.

Mum and Dad have clearly been discussing my
personal affairs with Grandpa, because he sat
next to me in the kitchen tonight while I was enjoying a bowl of type B+ and told me about an old
vampire saying that goes, "Beg for the take on
Sunday, beg for the stake on Monday." This means
that those humans who plead most desperately to
be transformed are always the ones who hate it
most. He said that any human who's giddy with

excitement about the prospect of turning vampire can't possibly understand what it means to be one.

I told him that we have a saying in our coven, which is, "Don't stick your nose in where it isn't wanted," and then I rushed upstairs to moan at Mum for sharing my personal information with others. As I was doing so, my sister poked her head around the door and asked if we were arguing about Chloe becoming a vampire. So she's been told too, has she? She can barely understand the emotional content of a Justin Bieber song, let alone complex issues like this. In future my personal problems shall go no further than this diary.

SATURDAY, OCTOBER 1
As I expected, Grandpa has filled my sister's small mind with fanciful notions, and now she's convinced she has extra vampire powers.

She came downstairs this morning and announced that she can now predict the future. A bit of a coincidence given that Grandpa was telling her about "vampire precognition" just a couple of days ago? Perhaps, but let's give her the benefit of the doubt. So how exactly does this power manifest itself? According to my sister, she was watching television this morning and she found herself knowing exactly what everyone was going to say.

Throwing my sister's claim open to scrutiny, I turned our TV to the news channel and asked her what the presenters were about to say. She made a couple of unimpressive guesses before stating that her powers weren't reliable yet because they were new.

After further interrogation it turned out that the TV show that had inspired the outbreak of precognition was an episode of *Friends* that had been on about fifty times before.

Quick, call the Vampire Council! My sister has the ability to remember lines from television shows she's seen before. What an amazing power, I don't think.

Hang on, I think I'm getting a vision of the future myself. I predict that my sister will convince herself that she has another special vampire power soon.

SUNDAY, OCTOBER 2
9:00 a.m.

I'm going round to Chloe's house again today, and if you must know, I'm rather excited because her parents are away again and I'm hoping to ditch all the boring transformation talk and get down to some good old-fashioned blood drinking.

If I add nothing more to my diary today, it's because we have shared a beautiful moment and I'm choosing not to divulge the gory details. And I certainly hope they will be gory!

10:00 p.m.

In retrospect, my suspicions should have been raised by Chloe's eagerness to let me drink her blood right away. Last time, we had a long chat first, and then I spent ages mesmerizing her, like you're supposed to do. This time she led me straight to a chair in her living room, which she'd surrounded with newspapers to protect the carpet. This wasn't quite the immortal dance of seduction I was expecting, but I wasn't complaining. She practically dragged me down to her neck and commanded me to start feeding.

I obliged as any cold-blooded male would have

done, but soon my enjoyment was compromised by a strange sensation in my arm. As a vampire, I can't really feel pain, but I still get a sense of when something is wrong, like a human would under a local anesthetic. I looked down at my forearm in horror to see that Chloe had slashed at it with a kitchen knife. Before I knew what was happening, she'd sliced along one of my veins and pulled my injured arm up to the two holes I'd made on her neck.

I could hardly believe that my beloved girlfriend, to whom I'd shown nothing but adoration, was trying to force a transformation. Just as I was

wondering how she possibly thought she could counter my strength, she squirted me in the face with a bottle of garlic-and-herb salad dressing. It hit me like Mace, and I dropped to the floor, overwhelmed by the horrible fug of parsley and dill.

What was she playing at? How could she possibly think this was a good start to eternity together? Immediately, I understood just how ugly the human lust for immortality can be.

As the dizzying effect of the garlic faded, I managed to wrench my arm away from Chloe's neck. She said it was too late, that I had already transformed her and there was nothing I could do about it.

I took no small pleasure in letting her know she'd been nowhere near close enough to death for the transfusion to work. I'd have had to feed on her neck at least five times longer for there to be any danger of her turning into a vampire. With that revelation, I went home and left her to contemplate her actions.

I think it's fair to say that our relationship has hit a hurdle.

1:00 a.m.

I've been considering Chloe's behavior today, and I'm afraid I can't bring myself to forgive her yet. I wouldn't say it's time for me to end things just at the moment, but her actions have made me seriously consider ever transforming her. If she's this impetuous at fifteen, imagine what she's going to be like at two hundred.

2:00 a.m.

Why do all these complicated things happen to me? I just want a normal life in a normal coven with a normal girlfriend. Everything always has to be a million times harder for me than for everyone else.

Sometimes I wish my parents had never transformed me and that I'd just been left to live a normal human life without any of the icy heartache or doomed longing of the immortal. Although, if that had happened, I'd never have lived to see high-definition TV, so I suppose it's about even, really.

MONDAY, OCTOBER 3

My shirt was covered in bloodstains thanks to Chloe's outlandish behavior yesterday, so I wanted to get to the washing machine this morning. However, it was already full because Mum was washing Grandpa's capes. I asked her why he couldn't do his own chores, and she said he was resting in his coffin and she didn't want to disturb him. Much as I predicted, Grandpa is exploiting vampire tradition to get out of housework.

Chloe was out sick today, which is hardly surprising. Although the makeshift transfusion she attempted yesterday won't provide her with any chance of turning into a vampire, it will certainly give her a serious headache.

I hope the time she spends in bed lets her reflect on her foolishness. She did a terrible thing yesterday, and if my parents ever found out about it, they'd ban me from seeing her again. It was very serious, and if I had any integrity as a vampire, I'd end things with her right now.

I might give her one more chance, though. She does have the prettiest neck in the school, after all.

TUESDAY, OCTOBER 4
9:00 a.m.

I shall be late for school this morning, as I'm still trying to process what has just happened. This morning a letter from Chloe arrived in the mail. I was expecting heartfelt regret, but what do I get?

Dear Nigel,

As you will have noticed, I am not in school today because of the blood loss I suffered on Sunday. Although I will apologize for trying to force you to transform me, I cannot apologize for wanting to become a vampire. It was really unfair of you to refuse to turn me because it made me feel left out. Because of this, I think it's better that we stop seeing each other.

I found it very frustrating to be so close to the vampire world without being allowed to join in, so it's probably better that I stay away from it altogether. I shall now return to my original plan of becoming an overseas volunteer and concentrate on my exams.

Sorry it had to end like this,

Chloe

Although I'm sad that my first ever relation-ship has crashed on the rocks of fate, the more I read this letter, the more I understand that Chloe wasn't ready for "the vampire world" at all.

Vampirism isn't a phase you go through, like wearing black nail polish or listening to Depeche Mode; it's a harsh reality that never ever stops. She says she felt "left out" because she wasn't a vampire. Has she any idea how "left out" you feel when you are one? Skulking around at night because you don't sleep, avoiding the sun because it hurts your skin, wearily watching the decades pass and the trends repeat and wondering if it might be better if a vampire slayer chopped your head off and put an end to it all.

It just goes to prove that all humans are

shallow, vapid, and foolish. I thought Chloe was different, but it turns out I was being foolish too.

6:00 p.m.

I sat alone in history and English today. I have now stopped feeling angry and started feeling sad about the abrupt end of our relationship. Although I keep reminding myself we had complicated issues, I can't help but feel rejected.

All day I swung back and forth from feeling disgusted with Chloe for the way she behaved to feeling disappointed with myself for not handling our problems better.

Why am I so pathetic that I should let a mortal affect me like this? To my kind, humans are meant to be little more than overdressed livestock. We're not supposed to brood over their every little action. Why can't I be a real vampire like Cagliostro of Sicily? They say his heartbreaking shenanigans in the seventeenth-century village of Erice caused so many women to commit suicide, they had to ship a boatload of women over from mainland Italy just to keep the place going.

Cagliostro

I was still lost in my reverie of regret when the drama teacher, Mrs. Stokes, approached me to say I was on at seven. At first I couldn't work out what she meant, but then I remembered the school talent contest. I tried to cancel, but before I could say anything, she dashed off. So now I have to put a mask of joviality over my heartbreak and go entertain the masses in the assembly hall. Still, I'll have no shortage of girls wanting to go out with me once they've seen my sexy backflip dance.

10:00 p.m.

I ought to revise my prediction about all the girls fancying me after my performance. In fact, I doubt I'll ever get a girlfriend again after that humiliating display.

I admit I was feeling slightly underprepared

as I waited in the "backstage" area, which Mrs. Stokes had created by draping some large red curtains over the balcony at the back of the hall, but I was still confident that my dance would bring down the house.

I peered through a gap in the curtains as all the teachers, pupils, and parents took their seats in the hall. Then Mrs. Stokes stepped out to introduce the first of the evening's acts, and it became apparent that I wasn't the only one who'd forgotten to rehearse.

Craig took to the stage and attempted to play the guitar solo from "Free Bird" by Lynyrd Skynyrd, but he kept getting it wrong and having to start again. By the time he finally got through it, the audience burst into applause, though it was more from relief than approval.

Then Mrs. Stokes took to the stage. She

always uses school talent shows as an excuse to inflict her singing on everyone, and she always goes on near the start so no one can leave. The song was called "Memory," from the musical Cats. If the idea of this musical was to replicate the noise of a cat howling in the night, it was certainly an accurate rendition.

Next, Gary and Nick from the lunch chess club recited Monty Python's parrot sketch. I can remember doubling up with laughter when I first saw this on TV in the late sixties, but in their flat, mumbled delivery, it seemed more like experimental drama than comedy.

Then Mrs. Stokes introduced me, and it was time to treat the audience to some real entertainment. I stepped out from behind the curtain and took my place on the stage. Mrs. Stokes clicked the play button on her laptop, and the opening bars of "I Like to Move It" blasted out of the assembly hall speakers. I bent my knees, clenched my fists and focused on the energy building inside me, just as I always do when I'm setting off my powers.

And then nothing.

Over the last few months unleashing my vampire powers has become as natural as breathing,

so I panicked when they didn't work. Determined to set them off, I shut my eyes, clenched my fists harder, and crouched down farther, desperately willing my body to flip in the air. It didn't help matters when a kid shouted something rude that set off a ripple of immature laughter.

By the time the song had finished, I'd still managed to do nothing except strain with the effort to set off my stupid powers. I opened my eyes and saw the whole crowd staring in embarrassment. Then Mrs. Stokes thanked me for a brave and challenging piece of performance art and gave a halfhearted clap. Nobody joined in.

As I left the hall, I was dismayed to hear that Jason's soccer skills display, which was merely an endless series of keepy-uppies, was drawing an enthusiastic response from the crowd.

Fine. Let these silly humans have their mindless entertainment. I'm through with trying to sink to their level.

WEDNESDAY, OCTOBER 5
12:00 p.m.

It seems I'm an outcast again. Everywhere I went this morning, callous students mimed a strained expression and made hilariously original comments like "Push, Nigel, push!" and "Have you tried laxatives?"

The irony is that as I don't eat or digest food. I can't suffer from constipation because I never poo at all. If anything, it's me who should be teasing those inferior humans about their repulsive digestive systems.

Worse still, it seems that Jason's pathetic "skills" display actually won the contest. Well, he's going to learn the bitter taste of defeat now. We're going out to Pottsworth Moor with the running club again this afternoon, and as soon as we're a safe distance from the group, I'm going to unleash my full vampire speed. I don't care if Dad punishes me for drawing attention to us. I have to do this. Time to make that monobrowed cretin eat my dust.

6:00 p.m.

I'm back from the run now, and I'm sad to report that Jason didn't have to eat any dust. In fact, he won the race comfortably. At first

we both stayed with the group, but Jason picked up the pace as we were coming to the first bend. I told my body to break into a sprint, but nothing happened. I just plodded along at the same pace as the rest of the group.

It was at this point that the desperation of my situation finally became apparent. Until I started going out with Chloe earlier this year, I had never been able to access my vampire strength and speed. And now that I've been dumped, my powers have gone.

I watched in horror as Jason and then the rest of the running club raced away. They were all sitting in the minibus ready to leave by the time I finally wheezed to the end of the course. I sat on my own at the front of the bus, scarcely able to admit to myself that I had become the world's most pathetic vampire once again.

THURSDAY, OCTOBER 6

It's official. Now that I'm single again, all my powers have vanished. Instead of going to school today, I went to the park and found that I couldn't lift anything heavier than a branch and couldn't run more than a few feet without having to catch my breath. I even tried to focus on a squirrel to see if my powers of animal control were still functioning, but it just stared back with a sarcastic expression on its face.

I sat on a bench and wondered how things could possibly get worse. Then I got my answer. I looked up and saw that I was surrounded by hundreds of dirty squirrels.

These vermin had been keeping a wise distance from me after I developed animal mind control earlier this year, but it didn't take them long to work out that I've now turned pathetic again.

I tried to leap over them, but they pounced on me and nipped with their horrible teeth. I dragged myself toward the edge of the park, swarming with the foul crea-tures as if I were wearing the world's least comfortable fur coat.

Eventually, I made it to the exit, and the horrid pests crawled off, lingering at the gates and baring their teeth.

My squirrel bites have healed now, but I must accept that the park is out-of-bounds once again. I'm going back to bed.

FRIDAY, OCTOBER 7

2:00 p.m.

The reality of single life is coming back to me now. The self-doubt. The isolation. The hopelessness. The eternal despair.

The one bright side to all this is that my poetic muse has returned. My emotional pain is the soil in which my word-flowers bloom. Here is my latest work. Take it, posterity. It's yours now.

BETRAYED

I thought you were different
But you're all the same
Greedy and selfish
And knowing no shame
If only I'd heeded
What Dad's leaflet said

106

I might lack a pulse
But you are truly dead

    Looking back over my poem, I can see that it carries a strong antihuman message, which might be offensive to some, but so what? Art expresses difficult truths. Deal with it.

9:00 p.m.

I tried to take my mind off my problems by going on the Internet tonight, but I only ended up making things worse by looking at Chloe's Facebook profile. She's already listed herself as single, and loads of her friends have clicked "Like" and written things like "U r better off without that loser" and "Men aren't worth it" on her wall. For your information, Facebook idiots, I'm a vampire and not a man. Not that

I'd expect accuracy from people who think the word "later" is spelled "L8R."

I can't even defend myself against these comments, because Dad won't let me sign up on Facebook in case everyone notices I don't get older. I even offered to age my profile picture every year with Photoshop, but he still refused.

I couldn't help noticing that Jason has made friends with Chloe on Facebook, because he writes "LOL xx" after all her status updates, even the harrowing ones about our breakup. I don't think it's right that someone as stupid as him should be allowed a computer. He'll probably try to use it in the bath.

To compound my irritation, Grandpa stuck his head round the door and complained that vampires my age have it too easy. He said that back in his day they didn't have computers, and if

they wanted to stalk someone, they had to get off their backsides and actually do it. I'm not stalking Chloe, I was just browsing through her photographs. And saving some to my hard drive.

12:00 a.m.

I had a headache tonight, so I went downstairs to tell Mum and Dad. They came out with the usual questions about whether I'd been drinking holy water or listening to Christian rock by mistake. I think I would have remembered that!

Grandpa took it upon himself to root around

my room and work out the cause of my illness. He came downstairs with a box full of "borderline religious items," including my copy of *The Lion, the Witch, and the Wardrobe*, which he said is actually about Christianity, and my *Star Wars* poster, which he said features a religion called "Jedi" that could give me mild headaches. So even pretend religions are bad for us now, are they?

So now I'm back in bed, still with a headache, but with lots of my favorite possessions in the trash. I think I'll keep it to myself next time I'm feeling under the weather.

SATURDAY, OCTOBER 8
10:00 a.m.

When I opened my curtains this morning, I noticed that the boy across the road has taped a poster for the local church youth group in his bedroom window. It features an image of Jesus on the cross and must be the real reason I had a headache last night. I knew Grandpa was talking nonsense about Star Wars. I tried to fish my stuff out of the trash, but Mum had thrown a load of stale blood away, so it was all ruined.

4:00 p.m.

Grandpa barged into my bedroom this afternoon and asked if I was feeling better. I said I was, just to get rid of him. He said if I was well again, then I should go out and get some exercise rather than moping around in my room. I said he didn't understand, which made him go off on a massive rant.

He said that vampires these days have gone soft and that I should try surviving off the blood of muskrats in a swamp for twenty years like he had to, then I'd have something to complain about. He droned on and on about how vampirism is a privilege and I was wasting it playing computer games when I should be out chasing girls. I told him that it was a privilege I hadn't asked for, and if there was a way of giving it up, I'd be more than happy to. He said that vampires these days didn't know they were dead, and I couldn't be bothered thinking of a clever reply so I shouted at him to get out of my room.

I have now made a KEEP OUT sign for my bedroom door. I know it's childish, and I haven't had to do it since my late fifties, but this is what he's driven me to.

A minor advantage to losing my girlfriend and my powers is that I can enjoy games again. I've just played a zombie cowboy game on the PlayStation for ten hours straight, and I intend to keep going until morning.

Sorry I was unfaithful to you when I had a girlfriend, PlayStation. While changeable women distract us with their empty pledges of love, you wait patiently on standby, knowing we will return to your comforts eventually.

SUNDAY, OCTOBER 9

10:00 p.m.

Mum and Dad made me

weed the front garden

this morning because it

was so unkempt and

overgrown that they

said it would draw

attention to us. I

told them that I was

happy for the weeds to stay there and remind

us all that nothing beautiful can ever prosper in

this drab world, but they weren't having it. I

wished they'd asked me a couple of weeks ago

when I still had my powers, as it took me ages

to finish, and Grandpa spent the whole time

peering down at me from his window. I bet it

was his idea.

What did I tell you? My sister has now decided she's got "telekinetic" vampire powers. She's clearly been listening to Grandpa's nonsense again, as she wouldn't have known the term for moving things without touching them if he hadn't told her.

I asked her for a demonstration, and she placed a pen on a sheet of paper on the living room table and made a big show of concentrating on it. She then used her vampire speed to whip the paper away so fast that the pen seemed to fly off the table.

My parents were incredibly impressed with this lackluster display. I pointed out that my sister was merely moving the paper quickly, but Mum said I should encourage her if she wants to learn magic tricks.

Okay, fine. Let's all fawn over my sister's

pretend vampire powers while completely failing to notice that I've lost mine due to emotional crisis.

Anybody care about that? Didn't think so.

7:00 p.m.

This afternoon I went to the Goth shop in the mall to get some new clothes. I bought a chain-mail shirt, black pants with tons of zippers, black eyeliner, and a skull earring. Mum was shocked when she saw my new outfit, but perhaps it will finally help her to understand how I feel on the inside.

I then tried to teach myself how to put eyeliner on, but I think I overdid it and made myself look like a raccoon. I tried to pierce my ears with the compass from my math set, but they kept healing up. I considered going back to the Goth shop to buy a clip-on earring, but I decided it was beneath my dignity as a supernatural being.

I don't care if Mum and Dad don't approve of my look. I finally look like a doomed prince of darkness who cares nothing for the rules of the mortal realm. Obviously, I'm not going to wear it to school, though. That would be asking for detention.

MONDAY, OCTOBER 10
2:00 p.m.

Chloe was back in school today. She sat with the tough gang in history, just so everyone would notice she was sitting apart from me. I thought the tough gang might refuse to let her sit with them because she told on them for giving everyone nosebleeds earlier this year, but they've already forgotten the incident because they're stupid.

I sat at a table with Katie and Jacqui, but whenever I tried to speak to them, they laughed between themselves like the fickle little humans they are.

Could it be that these are the same girls who were writing my name on their textbooks and using my face as a screensaver just a few weeks ago? It seems I'm just another faded teen craze like Buddy Holly, the Bay City Rollers, and the Backstreet Boys. Not that I care. I'm done with human girls—they're a total nightmare.

6:00 p.m.

Unless I accidentally called Domino's and ordered some extra toppings for my face, it looks as though my zits are back. Bright sunshine used to give me terrible acne, but when I got my vampire powers, it only gave me a mild rash. Now a cluster of whiteheads has appeared under my bottom lip, and whenever I try to squeeze them, my vampire healing powers make them grow right back. Thanks for that, healing powers. I thought you were supposed to help me, but I might have known you'd find a way of making things worse for me too.

11:00 p.m.

I asked Dad to help with my history homework tonight, but he wasn't any use. I was supposed to be writing about the causes of World War I, and I thought he might remember better than me, as I was only three at the time. But he just went on about how the evil vampire Dragoslav of

Serbia assassinated Archduke Franz Ferdinand and blamed it on someone called Gavrilo Princip in order to plunge Europe into war and make human blood more easily accessible.

Great, so I should just write that down and hand it in, should I? Because that's not going to arouse any suspicion, is it? I should have known better than to ask for Dad's help with history. While it's true that most humans believe in a whitewashed account of their past that makes no room for the undead, my homework is hardly the place to set the record straight.

TUESDAY, OCTOBER 11
1:00 p.m.

Chloe wouldn't sit next to me today, and she even looked the other way when I passed her in the corridor. Everybody seems to know that we've split up, so she must have been telling them because I haven't. Fine, let her spread her side of the story. I need to rise above these silly humans now.

Wayne, who went out with Chloe before I did, offered his commiseration to me during morning break. He said that she was a nightmare and that I was better off out of it. I felt like throwing him onto the roof of the science building for daring to compare my complicated romantic crisis to his shallow little feelings, but then I remembered I don't have my vampire strength, so I just shrugged.

The weird thing is that although I'm upset with Chloe for attacking me, I'd still consider taking her back if she begged me. At least it would mean getting my powers back. As it stands, I'm going to have to ask Dad to write a note excusing me from the cross-country club. Perhaps then he'll understand what I'm going through, although I won't hold my breath.

9:00 p.m.

I was writing the above diary entry in the library this lunchtime when I was distracted by a strong smell of disinfectant. I looked up and saw Gary, who uses Lysol rather than deodorant. He said that Keith's mother wouldn't let him come to school today in case he had a cold, so they were a man down for their lunch chess club. I thought it might take my mind off my emotional problems, so I agreed to join them in the room at the back of the library.

I played against Sanjay while Gary played against Nick. I was beaten quite easily, as I'm not great at chess. I don't know why I've never got round to learning it properly. I'm excellent at Battleship, Boggle, and Hungry Hungry Hippos, though.

The winners then played each other, and Sanjay was crowned the overall victor. I have to admit that their company proved a welcome distraction from my personal woes, even if they did keep making references to TV shows I don't watch like *Star Trek* and *Battlestar Galactica*.

I think I'll go to their club again tomorrow. I might even read up on chess tonight. It's not like I've got anything else to do.

WEDNESDAY, OCTOBER 12

What was I thinking?

I turned up at the chess club today with my head full of grand-master strategies, only to see that Gary was setting up a huge board covered in tiny squares. I asked him what was going on, and he said that they role-play on

Wednesdays instead of playing chess, as they all have notes to get out of PE and can play uninterrupted for four hours straight. Then Nick walked in carrying a replica *Lord of the Rings* sword. As I looked at them, I realized how far I'd fallen in such a short span of time. While it might be acceptable for a vampire to be tragic in the sense of brooding over lost love, it's not acceptable for a vampire to be tragic in the sense of owning dice with more than six sides.

I told them I had to get on with my class work and left.

6:00 p.m.

This afternoon I gave Mr. Moss my sick note. He looked disappointed that I was getting out of cross-country, so I pretended I'd been told to avoid running by the doctor. I then spent the rest of the day sitting in the library on my own, hoping that the strength and speed I enjoyed earlier this year weren't just part of a fleeting phase, but suspecting that they were.

THURSDAY, OCTOBER 13
6:00 p.m.

I decided to make friends with the school Goths—Brian, John, and Si—again today. I was anticipating a hostile response, as I tossed their friendship aside when I first started going out with Chloe earlier this year.

Sure enough, Brian went on about how I only wanted to be their friend again because I'd been dumped, while John just scowled silently. I let them have their little moment. It's all water under the bridge to me. Anyway, it's not technically right to say I was dumped because

I was considering calling it off with her. It was mutual.

Once they'd got it all out of their system, Si told me about the band they've formed, Feast of the Devil. I'm considering putting myself forward as a keyboard player, as I'm fantastic on the piano. I think I'd better listen to something they've written before I decide if they deserve me, though.

1:00 a.m.

There was a death-metal band called Mask of Sanity playing in a pub in town tonight, so I thought I'd go along to see what the kids are into these days. It turns out that what the kids are into these days is the man with long hair who works at Games Exchange doing an impression of Cookie Monster from Sesame

Street over some really loud guitars.

Speaking as someone who accidentally saw Jimi Hendrix live in a hotel in Scarborough in the sixties, I find it hard to get excited about modern music, but I had an enjoyable enough time. I even got up onstage and attempted to dive into the crowd, although they must have misunderstood my intention because they cleared out of the way. I crashed down to the sticky floor and broke my wrist, then had to hide it under my T-shirt while it was healing.

I tried to attract some Goth girls with mesmeric stares, but none of them were up for it. One of them even walked straight past me to a boy wearing a T-shirt with VAMPIRE written on it in a Gothic font. And here I was thinking that vampires drank human blood, not sodas. In

the end I decided to let these silly little girls

stick with their preening fakes and miss out on

the opportunity to experience the real thing.

It's their loss.

On my way home I couldn't stop my thoughts

from turning to Chloe. Perhaps I'm letting

myself get walked all over here, but I can't help thinking about how nice it would be if I could win her back and get my powers to return in the bargain. But what if she starts going on about transformation again?

Humans, eh? Can't live with 'em, can't live without drinking their blood.

FRIDAY, OCTOBER 14
6:00 p.m.

I looked for Chloe at lunch, but she was hanging out with Jason, Jay, Baz, and the rest of the tough gang. I hope she understands the company she's keeping there. Jay's dad was arrested last year for punching a bartender who tried to take away his glass while there was still some beer in it, and Baz has a record for spray-painting the golf club wall. He might have got away with

130

it if his graffiti tag wasn't his real name and address. Careful, Chloe, if you lie down with dogs, you'll end up catching fleas. I think there's still time to save her from the criminal life, though.

In the meantime, I went back to the Goths. I told them about how I went to see Mask of Sanity, and they seemed impressed. The discussion soon turned to their band, and I offered

them the benefit of my talents. They pretended to be reluctant, but you could tell they were excited by the artistic possibilities of our union, and they agreed to let me audition.

I have to confess I'm feeling rather stoked by the prospect of becoming a rock star. I might even use my vampire poetry skills to write their lyrics if I consider them worthy.

10:00 p.m.

My sister wouldn't shut up this evening about a lesson she'd had at school today about the environment. She asked my parents if they could hunt for blood closer to home to improve our carbon footprint, and they patiently explained to her that if we attacked humans round here, a vampire slayer or a fan of paranormal romance would track us down and there'd be all sorts of trouble.

If my sister doesn't approve of the way my parents harvest blood, she should go out hunting herself. After all, her vampire powers are much more reliable than mine. We should save the rations of blood in the fridge for those who can't feed any other way (and that doesn't include Grandpa).

2:00 a.m.

Following my sister's rant about the environment tonight, I've been wondering if it would make for a better world if our type took over.

If all the vampires of the world came out of the coffin and declared themselves to humanity, we'd be free to dash around at top speed without the need for pollutants such as cars and planes. And if humans got jealous and wanted to join us, we should let them. Before long, we would live in a vampire utopia, with all nations united under the rule of the Vampire Council.

Obviously, we'd have to make sure that at

133

least half the population stayed human; other-
wise, there'd be no one to feed on. And to
make things simpler, we'd probably have to keep
them in special camps surrounded by barbed wire.
But they'd be allowed food and toys, if they
behaved.

Actually, having considered it, that probably
wouldn't make the world a better place at all.
I don't like thinking about how to improve the
world. It gives me a headache.

SATURDAY, OCTOBER 15
6:00 p.m.

I brought my electronic keyboard down from the
attic this morning. It's older than I remembered,
and for some reason, it keeps breaking into a
bossa nova rhythm, which is unlikely to go down
well with the metal faithful. But once I'd

changed the tone from tuba to grand piano and practiced my Mozart pieces, I felt confident that my superior musicianship would win the day.

I arrived at Brian's garage just as they were setting up. I didn't think my battery-powered keyboard would have much of a chance against John's drums and Si's amp, and I was right. As they thrashed randomly away, I tried to add a keyboard line to the dirge, but I might as well have been tapping a marshmallow for all they could hear.

Brian started to scream a few minutes later, which I took as a sign that either he'd hurt himself or they'd finished jamming and were now playing an original composition. The song went on for about ten minutes without any sign of a chorus before Brian shouted "Satan!" and the instruments cut out.

When they did, I shouted "Keyboard solo!" and began to improvise a brilliant melody. I have to admit that I didn't do my contribution any favors by accidentally hitting the demo button, causing the machine to play "Together Forever" by Rick Astley in a series of novelty tones, but I still reckoned I'd proved I could lift the band to

the next level. So I was surprised when Si told me I'd failed the audition.

So I have now officially stopped being friends with the Goths again. I should never have offered the hand of forgiveness in the first place.

12:00 a.m.

I was on my way to the graveyard tonight to sulk about my failed music career when Jay and Baz from the tough gang stopped me and said I had to buy some alcohol for them. I'd have refused outright if Jason had been with them, but he wasn't, so I thought I might as well try to stay on the right side of the hard kids.

Jay and Baz gave me four dollars and shoved me into the liquor store. As I only ever drink blood, I don't have any experience buying alcohol, and the man behind the counter could tell I was uncomfortable. He peered up from his newspaper and asked if he could help. I panicked and grabbed a bottle of red wine, although Jay and Baz had actually requested beer. I think I was just drawn to the color.

I put it down on the counter, and the sales clerk asked for my date of birth. If I'd said my real one (May 14, 1911) the clerk would have assumed I'd had too much already, so I tried to calculate the date of birth of an eighteen-year-old.

The clerk recognized the strain of mental arithmetic on my face and told me to leave. But then I remembered I still had a library card from a few years ago inside my wallet, with my photo next to the date of birth May 14, 1991. I showed it to the guy, and he handed over the wine.

Outside, I gave the bottle to Baz, who thanked me despite looking disappointed at my choice of beverage. So I managed to stay friends with the tough gang, but the incident only heightened my concern about the company Chloe is keeping. It's only a short journey from underage drinking to taking drugs and selling your mum's jewelry or whatever it is that bad humans do.

SUNDAY, OCTOBER 16

My sister has now convinced herself that she has mind-reading powers. I asked her what I was thinking about, and she said, "Chloe." She was right, but that's because I'm predictable rather than because she's psychic.

I said we should try again, but this time I'd write down the name of the person I was thinking about on a piece of paper. Just to wind her up, I wrote "Kyle," the name of a boy from her school she fancies, and then decorated the paper with love hearts. She guessed that I was thinking about Grandpa, but when I revealed my answer, she launched into a violent attack. When I pointed out that as a psychic vampire, she must have known what I'd written and therefore would have no reason to become suddenly angry, she slumped back down on the sofa.

Much as I enjoyed all this, I'm disappointed it was so easy for my sister to guess who I was originally thinking about. I think I'll approach Chloe tomorrow. My terms will be that if she promises never to bring up the topic of transformation again, she can have me back.

MONDAY, OCTOBER 17

I waited outside the school gates for Chloe this morning to deliver my terms. She ignored me when she arrived, and I had to run after her and outline my conditions for taking her back. I hadn't got far when she interrupted me to say she had no intention of asking for my forgiveness, as she already had a new boyfriend!

I didn't quite know how to respond to this. I know we had our issues, but it's surely impossible to get over true love and move on to the next man in little more than a week! I was still reeling from this revelation when an event so unpleasant occurred that I can hardly bring myself to describe it. That lumbering, ignorant caveman, Jason, plodded around the corner and put his arms around Chloe. And then, instead of alerting a teacher, she gave him a kiss on the lips and said, "Hi, babe."

Then the oafish ignoramus had the nerve to hold his hand out to me and say, "No hard feelings." If I still had my vampire strength, I'd have lifted him up by that outstretched arm and flung him right through the windshield of the principal's car. As it was, I took the only sensible option and went home to bed.

TUESDAY, OCTOBER 18

I stayed in bed all day yesterday. I was considering doing the same today, but I'm determined not to let these shallow humans and their trivial little affairs get to me. I must remind myself that I'm from a superior species to Chloe's, and should be no sadder about losing her than a human would be about losing a pet hamster.

I might ask Grandpa if he knows any other

covens I could move in with. Then I'd be able to meet beings who've got more in common with me and perhaps find a nice vampire girlfriend. Or an evil vampire girlfriend. Either would do.

So I went to school today. I thought it would upset me to see Chloe and Jason walking around hand in hand, but it didn't really affect me. I saw them only five times—once in assembly, once in the corridor outside the science labs, twice by the bleachers, and once as they walked out of the school gates. I barely even noticed them.

Mum and Dad brought home some new thermoses of blood this evening, but they did little to cheer me up. The blood was a thin and tasteless type A-, and when I complained, they said that Grandpa has requested we drink healthier blood with lower sugar levels from now on. I told them that it was fine for him to go on a diet, but at my age I need all the energy I can get. I then demanded they go back out and harvest some sugary blood from the fattest person they could find before I collapsed with weakness, but I was ignored. Obviously.

WEDNESDAY, OCTOBER 19
12:00 p.m.

The word on the playground is that Chloe has been reported for dropping litter and stripped of class officer status. I knew she'd go bad when she joined the tough gang. Much as I predicted, she is now on the slippery slope to drug addiction and prison. Well, it's too late to save her now. She's ventured into the criminal underworld, and she's beyond my help.

9:00 p.m.

Tonight my sister showed us a paragraph about human rights that she's written (i.e., copied from the Internet) for her English class. It argued that everyone in the world, regardless of where they're from or how much money they have, has the right to live in a house and drink clean water and watch TV or whatever.

She seemed very pleased with it, so I thought I'd grill her further on the subject. I asked her if she thought it was a human right to go about your business without having your blood stolen from you. She said it was, then she thought about it for a minute and changed her mind.

145

Mum told me off for trying to confuse her, but it was a simple enough question. I just couldn't see why I should have to endure a lecture on the rights of humans given by someone who survives by drinking their blood. It's like being lectured on the rights of worms by a sparrow.

2:00 a.m.

Although I don't especially care about Chloe and Jason's childish romance, I can't help but feel as though I should get a new girlfriend to save face. But where can I find one? If I get involved with another human girl, she'll be overpowered by the same greedy lust for immortality that blighted my last relationship.

This is truly the curse of the vampire. You endure painful decades of loneliness until someone comes along who makes you think this planet might .

not be such a bad place after all, but then she goes immortality crazy, gets vexed when you won't transform her, and dumps you for a unibrowed oaf.

You see all those vampire fans mooning around with their pale foundation and black clothes, but if they had any idea what it's really like, they'd toss it in and take up stamp collecting instead.

For the time being, I'll just have to download a picture of a hot chick to my phone and pretend she's my new girlfriend.

THURSDAY, OCTOBER 20
12:00 p.m.

Craig saw the girl on my phone today and asked if she was my new girlfriend. I confirmed that she was, and he insisted on showing it to everyone in the class. Fortunately, I'd chosen an attractive woman, so I had nothing to be ashamed of.

Unfortunately, I'd failed to notice that the attractive woman in question was an actress from *Hawaii Five-O*. No wonder Craig laughed every single time I said she was my girlfriend.

When he pointed out that the girl was an actress, I said I must have used the wrong picture by mistake, but that didn't stop him from leading the entire class in a rendition of the *Hawaii Five-O* theme.

At lunch one of Darren's flea-ridden sneakers was thrown onto the roof of the science building. He's refusing to name his attackers, but rumors suggest that the tough gang was responsible and that Chloe was involved!

I know Chloe has recently suffered the breakdown of a serious relationship, but even a crisis of that magnitude can't explain how quickly she's gone off the rails. Just a few months ago she was thoughtful enough to lend Darren one of her father's tracksuits so he wouldn't have to suffer the indignity of coming to No Uniform Day with his PE gear on (he's too poor to own any other clothes). And now she's carried out an unprovoked footwear attack on him.

I can't help but feel partly responsible. If I'd given in and transformed her, she might not need to vent her frustration on the innocent. Though, on the basis of her recent behavior, I wonder if she might have turned into an evil vampire and killed loads of humans, and I'd have had all that on my conscience. You can't win.

6:00 p.m.
In math today I tried to sit as far away from Jason as possible and forget he was there. Unfortunately, when Mr. Wilson left the room, Jason disrupted the class with some boorish soc-cer chants.

I later informed Mr. Wilson and suggested that Jason should be expelled or, at the very least, put in another class. Mr. Wilson was unwilling to do so, as Jason's dad had threat-ened to "knock his block off" in a recent late-night argument at the Black Lion, and he

didn't want to do anything to aggravate the situation.

So this is how we're going to be ruled now, is it? By the threat of physical violence? Do two and a half thousand years of democracy and thirty years of Parent-Teacher Association meetings count for anything against the might of the brutes? Apparently not.

12:00 a.m.
I need to stop hating Jason so much. I've got to remind myself that he's a human and therefore not worth getting riled about. Like all his kind, he'll grow older and weaker until he turns to dust. Let him have his petty victories. He'll be gone in the blink of an eye, but I shall remain.

12:10 a.m.
It's not working. I still hate him.

FRIDAY, OCTOBER 21
1:00 p.m.
I went to Stockfield Moor for a stroll this morning, and I was surprised to see someone

running toward me at Olympic speed. At first I wondered if it was Jason, but as the figure approached, I saw that it was actually Grandpa! As soon as he spotted me, he slowed right down and clutched his back. I mentioned that he'd been running at a terrific pace, and he said that he'd been overdoing it and needed to go back to his coffin for a nice lie-down.

So much for Grandpa being frail. It looks to me like he's got perfectly functioning vampire powers. He just doesn't want Mum and Dad to know in case they make him pull his weight around the house and fetch his own blood rather than draining our precious resources.

2:00 p.m.

At lunch Jason got told off by Mr. Morris for kissing Chloe. Quite rightly too. Nobody wants to see disgusting kissing when they're trying to go about their business. Especially when it involves Jason with his rancid dog-meat breath. Just thinking about him put me off my lunch.

8:00 p.m.

We have a week off for break now, so it will be good to get away from all the petty school gossipers. I expect they'll have forgotten the whole silly affair by the time we get back. I know I will have.

SATURDAY, OCTOBER 22

2:00 p.m.

I was in the bookstore this afternoon looking at a "3-for-2" offer on vampire romance books when I had a brilliant idea. If everyone is going nuts for these cheap knockoffs written by opportunistic charlatans, imagine how they'd respond to a genuine work of undead insight by an actual vampire? Why am I wasting my powers of self-expression on poetry when I could be showing these bandwagon-jumping fools how it's done?

Of course, Dad will think I'm putting our identity at risk—blah blah blah, yadda yadda—but this is too good an opportunity to pass up.

6:00 p.m.

We need to keep Grandpa away from my sister because she believes any old nonsense he tells her. This morning I went into her room to get some blank paper, and she said

155

that vampires aren't allowed to enter the residences of others without formal permission.

For a start, that's just a stupid old superstition and only senile old vampires like Grandpa still bother with it. If my sister took just one second to think about it, she'd remember that she's been in hundreds of houses without asking for anyone's permission. And even if it were true, it wouldn't count for bedrooms. I told her that Mum and Dad own the entire house, including her room, but she was having none of it.

I attempted to prove my point by jumping back and forth across the threshold of the room, but unfortunately, I tripped over her Hello Kitty hairbrush and fell down the stairs, which she took as confirmation of her silly belief.

10:00 p.m.

I have now finished the first chapter of my book, *Dark Embrace of the Night*. It's pretty strong stuff, so if you don't want to be transported to a realm of dangerous passion, look away now. . . .

Dark Embrace of the Night

Chapter 1

Nathan walked into Claire's bedchamber, only to find her cowering in fear and wearing this flimsy white dress where you could totally see her neck.

"I'm afraid of you," whispered Claire. "So why is it I'm so attracted to you?"

"That's just the way it goes with me, babe," replied Nathan.

Then Claire swooned, but Nathan was used to it and didn't think it was that much of a big deal.

Nathan swooped down and they kissed for ages and then he got up to leave.

"Don't go," pleaded Claire. "I want you to drink my blood."

"Not on the first date," countered Nathan. Although she was massively hot, he didn't even care about her that much because loads of other fine girls fancied him anyway.

SUNDAY, OCTOBER 23
6:00 p.m.

This afternoon I had to go to a garden center with Grandpa to help him get some fresh soil for his coffin. I wanted to go to the one near the industrial park, but this would have meant crossing a river, so we had to walk all the way into town instead.* And guess who had to carry all the soil on the way back?

At one point a group of young boys asked us if we could kick their soccer ball back to them, and Grandpa whacked it with such force that it knocked one of them to the ground.

I shot him a suspicious glance to let him know that his display of strength hadn't escaped my attention, so he pretended to be tired for the rest of the way home. I might well have asked why a vampire with faulty powers was carrying three heavy bags of soil for a vampire with perfectly functioning ones, but I didn't think it was worth it.

---

*Another of Grandpa's doddery old beliefs is that vampires can't cross running water. Yes, they can—he must have done it thousands of times. I bet he crosses plenty of rivers and streams on long car journeys without even noticing. Plus, he claims Dad transformed him in nineteenth-century Paris, so he must have crossed an entire sea at some point.

I made good progress on my novel this evening:

Dark Embrace of the Night

Chapter 2

Claire found she had walked into the middle of a forest at night, though she had no idea how. Until, that was, she saw Nathan standing there and looking really cool in his Nike Air Max Previews, which are the most expensive sneakers you can buy in JJB Sports.

"I called you here," Nathan proclaimed sternly. He had the power of sending psychic messages to foxy chicks from miles away. It was just one of his special vampire powers, which included mind reading, flying, and firing lightning out of his eyes.

Claire drifted toward him as if he were a massive magnet and she were made of metal, but not a nonferrous metal like aluminum and copper, because magnets don't attract these, which we learned in science. She knew he was forbidden, outlawed, contraband, out-of-bounds, and off-limits, yet couldn't tear herself away.

"Heal my aching solitude," he growled sensitively.

Claire was just about to kiss Nathan, but then her boyfriend Jackson arrived, because he'd been following her, because he wanted to know who she was meeting so late at night.

I decided to leave Chapter 2 on this cliff-hanger, partly to keep the reader wanting more and partly because X Factor was starting. I made up the bit about vampires being able to fly and shoot flames from their eyes because I didn't want to give too much away about my species. Plus, wild exaggerations about our lot didn't exactly hinder Bram Stoker, did they?

MONDAY, OCTOBER 24

I had another good writing session today. I think focusing on the majestic realm of vampires is helping to remind me how trifling and insignificant the human world is.

Dark Embrace of the Night

Chapter 3

So Claire's boyfriend Jackson turned up in the moonlit forest just as she was about to kiss Nathan.

Jackson looked at the scene with confusion and anger. Although he was too stupid to understand exactly what was going on, he knew something was wrong.

"Get away from my girlfriend," he grunted.

"Why don't you come and make me?" retorted Nathan.

Jackson charged at Nathan and attacked him with all his brute strength. But get this—as well as being a sexy vampire, Nathan was also a ninja, and he totally beat him up.

"Thanks for totally beating him up," said Claire. "I've been wanting to dump that creep for ages, and seeing him humiliated like this is the perfect excuse."

"All in a day's work," said ~~Nigel~~ Nathan, and then he went off to help the government with some secret stuff because he was also a spy.

I decided to end the chapter there because I couldn't think of anything else to put in. But overall I'm very pleased with the way it's going.

TUESDAY, OCTOBER 25

I saw Jason and his family in town today, so I decided to watch them from a distance. It's not

that I'm obsessed with Jason, I just think my
vampire stalking instincts kicked in. Also, they look
like criminal types, so I thought I might see them
breaking the law and turn them in to the police.

I followed Jason and family down to the supermarket. They emerged ten minutes later with
four large bags that I initially took to be char-
coal but that turned out on closer inspection to
be dog biscuits. I couldn't recall Jason saying anything about owning a dog, which seemed odd. He
has a severely limited number of interests, so you
think he'd have mentioned it at some point.

If the family is keeping dogs in their cramped
house, they're almost certainly mistreating them.

I've decided to carry out further observation, and I won't hesitate to report them to the authorities if I uncover evidence of animal cruelty. Not that the animal kingdom deserves my help, of course. But if it helps to get Jason behind bars, it will be worthwhile.

LOG OF ACTIVITY OF JASON BROWN AND FAMILy FOR WEDNESDAY, OCTOBER 26:

7:30 a.m.
Jason's dad leaves the house, returns five minutes later with a lottery scratch card and a copy of the Star newspaper. A ginger cat arches its back and hisses as he passes.

166

11:00 a.m.

Jason's dad leaves the house to visit the barbershop. He emerges with very short hair. He buys a pack of razors and several cans of shaving cream from the drugstore on the way home.

1:00 p.m.

Chloe calls round for Jason, and they leave together, possibly for a romantic walk in the park. I reflect on the irrationality of the human race but resolve not to let it affect my observation of these idiots.

3:00 p.m.

Jason's mother and sister leave in the car.

3:30 p.m.

Jason's mother and sister return with four large bags of frozen meat, possibly from a wholesaler.

6:00 p.m.

I'm too thirsty to continue my stakeout today, so I'm abandoning my post for the night. I'll make sure to bring a thermos of blood tomorrow.

LOG OF ACTIVITY OF JASON BROWN AND FAMILY FOR THURSDAY, OCTOBER 27:

7:00 a.m.

Surveillance resumed.

7:30 a.m.

Jason's dad emerges from his house to buy a newspaper and scratch card and is again hissed at by the ginger cat. His hair seems to have regrown significantly since yesterday.

11:00 a.m.

Jason's dad leaves the house again. Although it is raining heavily, he neglects to wear waterproof clothing.

11:30 a.m.

Jason's dad visits the pet shop and emerges with two full shopping bags. Discarded receipt shows his purchases include flea powder and a rubber ball with a bell inside. Further evidence that the Brown family is keeping dogs, but where are they? And why are they hidden?

169

Could Brown family be involved in illegal dog-fighting contests?

Could Brown family be importing banned dogs such as the Japanese Tosa?

Could Brown family be breeding dogs to sell to local takeout joints?*

9:00 p.m.

Jason and family leave the house carrying plastic bags. Seems late for a family outing. Why the bags?

9:30 p.m.

Chloe calls round at the empty house. She rings the buzzer several times before shouting through the mail slot.

---

*Craig once told me that some takeouts save money by abducting stray dogs and cooking them, but having once tried to catch a Labrador in order to drink its blood, I can confirm that it would be much easier to buy meat from a shop, so I find this unlikely.

9:35 p.m.

Chloe walks away from the house looking disappointed.

11:30 p.m.

Jason and family still haven't returned. I suspect
he's involved in underage drinking.

1:30 a.m.

They're still out. The possibilities are becoming
increasingly unsavory. Nightclubbing? Carjacking? Cow
tipping?

2:30 a.m.

Still no sign of Jason and family. Post abandoned
due to remote possibility that my parents are worried about me.

LOG OF ACTIVITY OF JASON BROWN
AND FAMILY FOR
FRIDAY, OCTOBER 28:

7:00 a.m.

Surveillance resumed. The curtains in the house are now drawn. I surmise that the family has returned.

3:00 p.m.

The curtains are now open, but there seems to be little activity. Stakeout proving boring. Tempted to buy a newspaper but worried about missing vital clues.

10:00 p.m.

Brown family leave the house, once again carrying plastic bags. This time I will follow them.

11:00 p.m.

Brown family walk for just under sixty minutes, ending up on west side of Pottsworth Moor.

11:30 p.m.

Brown family are sitting in an area of open moorland and preparing for some sort of midnight picnic. The plastic bags contained spare clothes and raw meat. The clothes have been buried in the ground, while the meat has been piled in the middle of the clearing. I am hiding in some bushes a few feet away from them. Luckily, the moon is full, so I can see very clearly.

12:00 a.m.

Help!

1:00 a.m.

Can't write. Must keep running.

1:30 a.m.

I don't want to die! I've got so much to live for! I haven't even unlocked the second island on Grand Theft Auto yet.

2:00 a.m.

If these are my last words, I'd like to thank my parents for everything, despite what I might have said in the past. I'd also like to make it absolutely clear that my sister should not take possession of my computer, television, games consoles, or collection of novelty thermoses.

SATURDAY, OCTOBER 29

It is now Saturday afternoon and my hands have stopped shaking, so I can write about what happened yesterday.

I observed Jason and his family from my hiding place in the bushes until just after midnight,  when the clouds parted to reveal the full moon. All the members of the Brown family then adopted a strange position, crouching down with their heads pointing to the sky. I was puzzling over this when their noses stretched into hideous snouts and the veins on their necks thickened into bulbous tubes. Their backs arched until they were horribly stretched and their legs and arms snapped into disgusting haunches. Their clothes were ripped apart as thick hairs forced their way out of their sore flesh and the vertebrae on their backs popped up one by one. Their fingernails grew into yellow claws and their painful cries became animal howls.

I won't lie. I was frightened. Let's just say that if I were the urinating type, I'd have needed a change of trousers. You might think it's pathetic for a vampire to be scared of werewolves, but I didn't even know they were real. Dad had mentioned them a few times, but he talks so much rubbish, I thought he was making it up. Plus, I've always had a particular dislike of dogs, so I found the sight of Jason and his family transforming into canines especially vile.

As soon as they'd transformed, they dug into their meat. They were engrossed in their disgusting raw scraps, so I thought it might be a good time to make my escape.

Unfortunately, I cracked a branch with my foot, and the Jason werewolf peered round. The wolves padded toward me, leaving aside their scraps for fresher meat. Jason broke away from the pack and pounded forward. Had he spotted me?

I flung myself into a ditch and covered myself with handfuls of soggy leaves. Luckily, Jason was as stupid in wolf form as he is in human form, and he bolted right past me. His pack ran after him, and soon the thud of their paws passed into the distance. I crawled out of my ditch and glanced up at the top of the hill to see the foul beasts ripping apart a lamb.

Now that I'm back indoors, I have begun to

fear for poor, vulnerable Chloe. How trustingly she has given herself to these monsters. How can I reach her before they do to her what they did to that innocent lamb?

SUNDAY, OCTOBER 30
6:00 p.m.
My family went out for a hike this afternoon, but I stayed behind to snoop around Dad's study for information on werewolves. The only thing I could find was a decrepit old book called *Defeating the Lycanthrope Menace.*

I'm sure the book is biased, but it sounds like I ought to keep quiet about my discovery. It says that vampires and werewolves have been deadly enemies for centuries, that there have been countless bloody wars between them, and that if a vampire encounters a werewolf, they must inform their coven so they can battle it immediately.* In other words, if I open my mouth, I'll be volunteering for a violent supernatural showdown that will most likely result in my head getting chewed off. Combined with the stress of my practice SATs, that would be too much.

On a more reassuring note, the book said that werewolves transform only on the three nights of the month when the moon is fullest, so I think the Brown family will now stay human until next month. At any rate, I think I should abandon my surveillance. It's not that I'm scared. It's just that I'm behind with my course work.

---

*According to the book, the phrase "cry wolf" comes from the story of a vampire in ancient Greece who would often pretend werewolves were attacking him as a practical joke. So when he really was beheaded by one, his coven ignored his cries for help. To some, the moral of this story is that no one believes a liar even when he's telling the truth. To others, the moral is that most people will ignore the sound of a practical joker being killed.

12:00 a.m.

I'm not sure it's safe for me to continue this diary. If a human ever got hold of it and found out about the war between vampires and werewolves, I'd get in all sorts of trouble. I think I'll continue it in Ancient Vamperian to be on the safe side.

MONDAY, OCTOBER 31

Actually, writing in Ancient Vamperian was too much effort. I had to keep consulting Dad's dictionary because I'd forgotten the hieroglyphs. I think I'll switch back to English, but I'll be sure to keep this diary with me at all times.

I was back in school today, and I spent the whole time trying to avoid Jason. I must admit I got a bit nervous whenever I was near him, and it didn't help that the halls had been decorated with frightening Halloween decorations. You might think that crude paintings of witches, pumpkins, and skeletons would be no problem for a supernatural entity, but after my recent experience I was feeling very fragile and sensitive.

When it's Halloween, we usually turn the lights off and pretend to be out, but tonight Grandpa is opening the door and dishing out candy to anyone who comes to the door. I think he's enjoying wearing his huge purple cape without raising suspicion.

I have to admit it made me nervous whenever someone in a werewolf mask rang the bell. There's no way they could know that I'd recently had a dangerous encounter with a pack of them, but I still find it insensitive. If someone was knocked down by a Harley-Davidson, you wouldn't turn up at their house the next day dressed as a motorbike and expect them to give you candy.

It was interesting to watch my sister's reaction to the various Halloween costumes, because it showed just how little she's learned in her nine and a half decades on this planet. She said she liked the "Frankingstein" the best, and I made an effort to explain that Frankenstein was the name of the scientist, not the monster, but it didn't sink in. Then she said she hated the "skel-lington" most, because it was the most fright-ening. I asked her if she was aware she had a skeleton inside her own body. She freaked out and shouted that she was a vampire, not a "dis-gusting skellington." My parents overheard the fight and yelled at me for trying to worry her. If anyone deserves telling off, it's her for spend-ing the better part of a century in education without developing even a basic grasp of anatomy. But nothing's ever her fault, of course.

TUESDAY, NOVEMBER 1

Today I spent all of math class glancing

fearfully at Jason. At least these diabolical events have proved I'm not paranoid. My instincts told me there was something wrong with him, and my instincts were right. On the other hand, how am I supposed to rearrange equations when I'm so near to a merciless killer who would rip my throat out if the lunar cycle demanded it?

I suppose it explains why he didn't understand Animal Farm. When you live in a family of wolf-people, it must be easy to misinterpret a book about talking pigs, horses, and goats as gritty realism.

According to Dad's book, the best way to kill a werewolf is to shoot it with a silver bullet. Maybe I could buy a gun and four silver bullets on eBay, sneak into Jason's house at night, and finish off his sordid clan, one by one. My problems would be over, and I might even win Chloe again and get my powers back.

No, I mustn't think that way. I'm better than that. Blood-guzzling fiend or not, I won't resort to violence. It's better to resolve problems through diplomacy. Or ignore them until they go away.

WEDNESDAY, NOVEMBER 2

I tried to find Chloe at lunch to warn her about Jason, but she was nowhere to be seen. Even though she rejected me for that lumbering fool, she deserves better than to end up as dog food.

Some people might think she was in danger when she was going out with me, but it's much more serious now. When she was hanging around with my coven, she was in danger of getting her neck pierced in a couple of places. But if she turns up at Jason's house on the wrong night, she'll get the whole thing chomped off. I admit that vampires are a minor health hazard for humans, but she's really messing with the wrong crowd this time.

THURSDAY, NOVEMBER 3

Chloe was back in school today, but she was with Jason every time I saw her, so I had to tape a note to her locker instructing her to meet me on the playing fields tomorrow. I hope she survives until then.

At lunch I overheard a group of kids play-ing a horror-themed version of Top Trumps. I thought I'd misheard when one of them shouted that werewolf beats vampire on strength, so I asked to examine the cards. Sure enough, the cards give werewolves a physical strength rating of nine, while vampires get a measly eight.

I have no problem with the makers of Top Trumps releasing a supernatural version of their game. I can even forgive them for mixing real species such as my own with imaginary beings such as Godzillas and Mothras, whatever they are. But if they want their game to be credible, they must ensure that the vampire card scores higher in every category than all the other cards.

I shall now write to the manufacturer of the game and suggest a few changes:

Vampire	
Beauty	10
Strength	10
Speed	10
Style	10
Poetry	10
Ability to read books without speaking the words aloud	10

Werewolf	
Beauty	1
Strength	8
Speed	7
Style	2
Poetry	0
Ability to read books without speaking the words aloud	0

FRIDAY, NOVEMBER 4

2:00 p.m.

I've had my meeting with Chloe now, and to be honest, I'm wondering why I ever wanted to save her.

She turned up half an hour late and told me that if I wanted to go out with her again, I was wasting my time. I said that nothing could be further from my mind and I had only asked to speak to her because her very life was in danger. I expected her to beg me to continue, but she merely tutted as if I were telling her off for littering.

I related the events of last Friday night, dropping my voice to a discreet whisper. I was just getting to the bit where I hid in the bushes, when Chloe interrupted me to say that if this was about Jason being a werewolf, she already knew and didn't see how it was any of my business.

I truly didn't know how to react to this. We're talking about a family who stalks the hills and eats defenseless animals, perhaps even humans, too. I pointed this out, and she asked how exactly this was different from what my family members get up to.

Unfortunately, her equation of graceful, elegant vampires with sweaty, grunting fleabags touched a nerve, and I'm sad to say that our conversation descended into childish insults. I said that at least I didn't smell of dog, like Jason. She said that she'd rather go out with a dog than an old bat. I retaliated by asking if supernatural beings were her type and whether she was planning to go out with a demon or a poltergeist next. She said that either would be more fun than me and stormed off. If she ends up as a pile of bones at the bottom of Jason's dog bowl, I shall have no sympathy.

8:00 p.m.

I'm finally done with human women. You give them a chance to consort with beautiful immortals and they choose smelly mutts instead. How dare she mention me in the same breath as those vile mongrels? He doesn't even have opposable thumbs every day.

It's fine. I'm over it. The end.

4:00 a.m.

I have now finished my novel, *Dark Embrace of the Night*:

"Why won't you stay with me forever?" begged Claire. "I thought you cared for me."

"Maybe I do," countered Nathan. "Maybe that's why I never want to see you again."

Nathan was used to this kind of hassle. He always warned girls that they couldn't be with him forever, and he always broke their hearts.

"Don't cry, babe," soothed Nathan, wiping away a tear from Claire's luscious cheek. "I can't be tied down to one chick. You know that."

"So why did you save my life by killing that army of werewolves?" asked Claire.

"Because werewolves are a threat to everything good and right in this world, and they must be stopped. If my story has any kind of message, that would be it."

On that important note, Nathan flew off into the dark embrace of the night.

THE END

My book has twenty chapters in total. It's a white-knuckle roller-coaster ride with plenty of twists and turns and will be a surefire smash. I have now stapled it together and sent it to a publisher, and I will think about it no more until I have received a serious offer from them.

SATURDAY, NOVEMBER 5

I went to the top of Pottsworth Moor tonight so I could see all the fireworks displays for miles around. It was the first time I've been back since the wolf incident, so I was rather nervous, and some of the louder bangs made me jump. But

I reminded myself that Jason and his vile pack won't transform again until the full moon at the end of this month, so I wasn't in any danger. Plus, pets have to stay indoors on Bonfire Night.

Now that my novel is completed, I'm free to turn my skills to poetry again. Tonight I wrote a piece that uses fireworks as a metaphor for doomed love. It features alliteration, which is when you use several words beginning with the same letter. Mr. Byrne taught us this in English, though he used an Eminem rap rather than a poem as an example so thick pupils like Jason wouldn't think he was uncool.

FIREWORKS

Our love was a rocket

Burning bright and brief

Our love was a Catherine wheel

Spinning with sudden sparks

Our love was a sparkler

Fizzing with fleeting fire

But now our love has malfunctioned

And like a faulty firework

We must never return to it

SUNDAY, NOVEMBER 6

Mum barged into my room this morning and announced that we were all going to the seaside. Grandpa said he couldn't come because his back was giving him trouble, no doubt planning a full day of glugging our blood supplies.

The weather turned while we were driving there, and by the time we'd parked the car, it was pouring. Everyone was disappointed by this, but I was pleased that the weather was as bleak and turbulent as my state of mind.

Dad said he didn't want to leave the car because his cape might get wet. I thought the point of capes was to protect you from the elements. Why buy one so expensive that you can't even use it?

I let them wait in the car while I walked along the rain-lashed shore and watched the crashing waves, which were as changeable and unstable as humans. (Note to self: Is there a poem in this?) By the time I got back to the car, my family had drunk all the blood we'd brought along, so I had to go thirsty.

I don't know why they can't exercise even a tiny amount of self-control. Dad clearly drank too much, because he kept changing lanes without signaling on the way home, and we were honked at several times. And my sister drank so much that we had to pull over on the hard shoulder for her to vomit. I saw a few car passengers look on with horror as they sped past, witnessing what they took to be an injured young girl bleeding profusely from the mouth (rather than a greedy young vampire with no one to blame but herself).

MONDAY, NOVEMBER 7
1:00 p.m.

My recent encounter with the wolves must have played havoc with my nerves. When I went to the bathroom this morning, I thought there was a zombie stumbling down the corridor toward me. It turned out to be Dad, who was hung over from all the blood he drank yesterday.

It's hardly surprising that I'm having these nervous episodes. Until a couple of weeks ago, I didn't even know werewolves were real. It wouldn't surprise me if flesh-eating zombies turned out to be real too and took over the world.

I hope they don't, though. Their blood must taste *really* stale.

11:00 p.m.

I got home tonight to find that the table had been set. When I asked what was going on, Grandpa said he wanted us to sit around the dinner table and drink as a family more often. Great. So now that old fool gets to dictate how I behave in my own house, does he?

It was really awkward having to drink with the family instead of alone in front of my PlayStation. Mum poured the blood into an ancient pot and ladled it into bowls, creating unnecessary dish wash-ing that I'll no doubt get saddled with. Grandpa wouldn't let anyone touch their blood until we'd all said "Bless the sacred life force," which is some pointless old vampire tradition, and then he slurped his blood in a really loud and annoying way.

Dad asked me how school was, and I said it was fine. He asked me if I was prepared to elaborate, and I said I wasn't. Grandpa told a story about the Crimean War that seemed to go on longer than the war itself. I know it was a difficult time, but it was over 150 years ago. He needs to let it go.

The only thing that made the entire dreary experience bearable was that Mum and Dad had harvested some delicious type AB+ for the main course and some thick, sugary type B+ for dessert. Yum.

When we'd finished, Mum pretended it had been nice and announced that we'd do the same again tomorrow. So now I have to waste time with these boring old corpses or I won't get fed, which is little short of blackmail. As soon as I get my powers back, I'm going to move into a place of my own, just you wait.

200

TUESDAY, NOVEMBER 8

I haven't heard back from the publisher yet, which is strange. They should have the novel by now.

I had to suffer more of Grandpa's stories during family mealtime tonight, although he did say one interestingly gross thing, which was that they used to keep cattle in the cellar of a coven he once lived in. I was going to ask him why anyone would go to the trouble of having noisy cows in their house all day and night when I realized he was actually talking about keeping humans for their blood!

I have to say I'm shocked that a race as sophisticated as ours could sink to such barbarism. If anything like that ever happened here, I'd have to leave immediately on moral grounds, as I'm a liberal. I'll be the first to admit that having an unlimited supply of delicious, fresh blood would be handy, but I do have something called a conscience, you know. I doubt any of this lot have heard of it.

WEDNESDAY, NOVEMBER 9
2:00 p.m.

Still no word from the publisher. I called their offices today, but they were all in a meeting. Even the receptionist had to go to the meeting when I tried to explain the novel's symbolism to her.

I saw Chloe sitting with the tough gang again at lunch. She was clutching a book, an object that no doubt confused the rest of the group. It was called *Taken by the Night Hunter*, and as far as I can tell, it's a new book in the Dark Temptations series that's about werewolves rather than vampires. Yeah, I'm sure it's really romantic when they declare their eternal love for you with Pedigree Chum breath.

Maybe I shouldn't be so hard on wolfpeople, though. Because you know who the vilest creatures of all are? Humans, that's who. Callous, fickle humans. I'd happily see the lot of them wiped out by a virus if they weren't so tasty.

10:00 p.m.

Grandpa told me off for using a swear word during family mealtime tonight. If he wants me to participate in his ridiculous charade, he needs to let me be myself. It's bad enough having to sit through his boring stories without having to worry about censorship whenever I open my mouth. I tried to give the old fool a bit of perspective by pointing out that we were a group of damned creatures drinking the blood of innocents, so foul language ought to be the least of our worries. He said that I was a self-hating vampire and that I should ram a stake into my heart if I was so ashamed of what I was, completely missing the point, as usual.

In the end I took my bowl of blood up to my room and announced that I wouldn't be attending any more family mealtimes. And to show them I meant it, I unleashed another swear.

THURSDAY, NOVEMBER 10
8:00 p.m.

I got home today to find that another vampire has been added to our overcrowded coven! Her name is Ivana, though I'm told I must refer to her as "Auntie Ivana." Apparently, she's a friend

of Grandpa, and she's come over from Poland. Thanks for asking our permission, Grandpa.

Ivana is very attractive, which is probably why Dad let her stay, but I find her rather odd. She keeps making jokes that don't make sense and then laughing really loudly, so you have to join in just to be polite.

1:00 a.m.

Things have gone too far this time. According to Dad, Ivana is moving into my room and I've got to share my sister's room for the foreseeable future. This is an infringement of my human rights. Or at least my supernatural rights.

205

If they had any understanding at all, they'd know I need my space now more than ever. When you're going through an emotional crisis, the last thing you need is to be subjected to ridiculous teen pop and inane phone conversations.

FRIDAY, NOVEMBER 11
6:00 p.m.

This is truly unbearable. I am trying to write these words from a mattress in the corner of my sister's room, but the terrible music she's listening to on her computer's tinny speakers is rendering it impossible. I'm sure that manufactured pop is another thing that I'm allergic to, like garlic and crucifixes.

She keeps watching the same music video of a young boy dancing with models in front of a pool over and over again. I asked her to stop, but she said she'd joined a campaign to make it the most watched video in the history of YouTube. I find it astounding that someone who lived through World War II would consider that a worthwhile cause.

Why does my sister fall for all this nonsense? You'd think she'd have seen it all before: rebellious fifties rockers, long-haired seventies idols, nineties boy bands. But every time the next big thing comes along, she gets smitten all over again.

I can't cope with it anymore. I'm going to demand that my parents give me my room back and kick Ivana out. If they insist on letting all these other vampires stay, I won't be here to put up with it. It's me or them.

8:00 p.m.

I just gave my dad the choice between me and the other vampires, and he chose them. To be honest, I think he'd had a bit too much to drink, because Ivana was showing him how to mix a cocktail with type A- and type B+. He went off on a rant about how I should lighten up and stop thinking about things too much.

What exactly does he mean by "thinking about things too much"? As far as I'm aware, my mind operates pretty constantly. I can't control its rate of activity. Do other people have a switch to turn their minds off when they're tired of thinking? It would explain an awful lot.

Perhaps Dad will regret his words when I'm gone, perhaps not. At any rate, I've decided to run away. I've packed a change of clothes and a few thermoses of blood, emptied my piggy bank, and left the following note:

Dear So-Called Parents,

It's only fair of me to inform you that I'm leaving our coven after eighty-five years. Although I'm grateful for all the blood you've harvested for me during this time, I feel that our situation has now become unworkable and that the time has come for me to leave. In particular, I find it unacceptable that I should have to share a room with my sister.

The coven is expanding for the first time since I joined it, with the addition of "Grandpa" and "Auntie Ivana." In the light of this disruption, I'm leaving to fend for myself. Please don't try to contact me.

Nigel

P.S. Don't let my sister trick Ivana into swapping bedrooms with her. She's had her eye on that room for ages.

P.P.S. When clearing out my room, do not throw away any of my poems, as they will be valuable one day.

So this is it. I'm now waiting at the Stockfield station for the late train to London. I'm so convinced about my plans, I've bought a one-way ticket, even though round-trip would have been just ten pence more.

I'm leaving behind this small town with its ridiculous werewolves and vampires. Let them discover each other and battle to the death for all I care. I wouldn't even know which side to support right now.

Perhaps I'll find a new coven, or perhaps I'll start one of my own by transforming loads of hot girls with long necks. Either way, this is where the next chapter begins.

12:00 a.m.

I am now staying in the cheapest bed-and-breakfast I could find near King's Cross Station. The whole room is sticky, and the walls are so thin, I can hear a man three rooms away snoring, but the freedom of finally leaving my stifling coven more than makes up for the discomfort.

I got bored on the train journey and drank all my blood supplies, so I'm going to have to go out and hunt tonight. But that's okay. I'm over one hundred years old, so it's about time I worked out how to do it.

Here I come, mortals. Fear me.

2:00 a.m.

To be honest, my first attempt at hunting didn't go very well. I've just returned from a nightclub called Voltz, but I didn't manage to feed on anyone. When most vampires go to clubs or bars, they just have to lurk in a corner and stare moodily, and their supernatural beauty does the rest. Since my vampire attractiveness has gone away again, I had to buy a novelty book of come-on lines from the station book-shop.

Whoever wrote it clearly didn't know what they were talking about, though, because I couldn't get a single line to work. I approached the girls in the club in order of attractiveness and read out lines like "The only thing your eyes haven't told me is your name" and "Shall we talk now or continue flirting from a distance?" None of them asked if they could come back to my room, and most of them didn't even let me read to the bottom of the first page.

To be fair, the music was very loud, so they might not have been able to hear my seductive words. I might go to the McDonald's across the road to try again.

3:00 a.m.

 I sat down in the corner of the fast-food restaurant pretending to drink a Coke. Before long, an attractive woman strode toward me. A little older than I'd been hoping for, perhaps, but still a good catch. I didn't have time to find my book of come-on lines, so I had to fix her with a mesmerizing stare instead.

It was working. She was coming over to me. This was it.

She asked if I was all right and if I'd lost my mum. My mum? I was hypnotizing her with smoldering, intense passion. What did my mum have to do with anything?

In a last-ditch effort to seduce her, I leaned

forward and attempted a kiss. She slapped me and told the manager, and I was thrown out of McDonald's.

I must now resort to attacking my prey. This isn't going to be pretty, but if that's the way humanity wants it, that's the way humanity shall have it.

SATURDAY, NOVEMBER 12
8:00 a.m.

I assumed my vampire stalking instincts would kick in if I followed people, but it was harder than I expected. I just couldn't bring myself to pounce on anyone. I must have too much of a conscience, I suppose. I followed a woman for a while, but just as I was about to leap on her, she called her husband to let him know she was safe, and I couldn't do it.

I sat down in the doorway of a kebab shop and tried to build my confidence by repeating, "I am a frightening supernatural being. I can do this." Eventually, I psyched myself up to attack. In retrospect, it was foolish to pick a woman who looked like she was a professional wrestler. Even if I'd been strong enough to overpower her, I'm not sure my fangs could have penetrated her neck muscles.

She slammed me to the floor, stamped on my stomach, and called me a pervert. I waited for my ribs to heal and returned to my bleak hotel room alone.

10:00 a.m.

I'm getting a headache now. I must have drunk too much on the train down here. I can't do anything until my hangover shifts, but I'll surely have more success if I go out with a clear head tonight.

9:00 p.m.

I have now gone almost an entire day without blood, and I'm getting overwhelmed by thirst. If this is how vampires in the old days used to feel, it's no wonder they behaved so unpleasantly.

I must now throw ethical concerns aside and take blood where I can find it. I will prey on the weak and vulnerable and even on the injured. This is what I must do to survive. This is who I am.

SUNDAY, NOVEMBER 13
9:00 a.m.

Well, I'm back from another unsuccessful night of hunting, and I can now see spots in front of my eyes.

Even preying on the weakest members of

society proved too hard for me. I jumped on what I took to be a child. Unfortunately, it turned out to be a very short woman who was trained in self-defense. She pulled me into a headlock and I didn't have the strength to wriggle out, so I had to resort to tickling her, which was truly pathetic. I bet Dracula never had to tickle anyone.

After that, my confidence was gone and I couldn't bring myself to attack anyone. Eventually, I spotted a man passed out on a bench next to some empty cans of lager. His head was slumped back, leaving his jugular vein exposed, so it looked like an easy feed. Unfortunately, the stench of alcohol was so strong that my fangs wouldn't extend. I stood there uselessly for a few minutes before returning here.

The shops were opening again by then, so I stopped off at a supermarket and bought a raw steak. It still had a small amount of blood left in it, but it was totally stagnant. I need fresher blood soon or I'm going to be in serious trouble.

5:00 p.m.

I'm now so weak, I can hardly lift my pen. This afternoon I went into a pet shop to buy an animal and drink its blood. Every creature in the shop erupted into a frenzy as soon as I entered, so I had to wait outside and ask someone to go in for me, like Jay and Baz do outside the liquor store. I gave a man fifty pounds and asked him to buy the biggest animal he could. I was expecting a Doberman or Rottweiler at the very least, but the best he could manage was two gerbils. And he kept the change.

I've been back in my room for the past hour, trying to feed from the gerbils, but so far I've used up more strength chasing them than I ever would have got from their stupid blood. They've been flinging themselves around the room, running under the bed, and hiding behind

the radiator. I even tried to use animal mind control on them, but they just sneered back.

So this is it. I'm too weak to hunt for more blood, so unless a cleaner with a nosebleed enters my room anytime soon, I'll now enter the final stages of vampire starvation. They say starvation can't kill us, but our bodies shut down so fully that humans assume we're dead and bury us alive. Great. That's one to look forward to, then.

I'm signing off now, as my pen feels as heavy as an axe. I hope I managed to add a little to the world's knowledge of my species. I wonder if I'm really damned to hell. If so, it seems a bit harsh. It's not like I asked to become a vampire. I did steal my sister's Angelina Ballerina pencil sharpener that time, though.

Fading now. Good-bye, world.

MONDAY, NOVEMBER 14
6:00 p.m.

Thankfully, I'm not writing this from inside a coffin under six feet of soil. After I completed the above diary entry, my body seized up and I lay motionless until morning. Vampire starvation was worse than I could ever have anticipated, as I had an itch on my leg and I couldn't get to it. The gerbils must have figured out something was up because they emerged from their hiding place and nibbled on my feet, causing more unreachable itches. This torture went on until the maid came in the next morning. She screamed for the manager, who looked at my paralyzed body and the gerbils and asked what the hell I'd been up to.

It was quite difficult for me to make out what was happening, as I couldn't move my head, but as far as I could tell, I was placed on a stretcher and taken to the hospital in an ambulance. I was then left on a stretcher in a corridor. I started to fret that a doctor would inspect me, realize I'm a vampire, and tell the papers. I think it was this fear that spurred me to lift up my head.

The patient on the gurney next to me had a bag of blood attached to his arm. The tangy smell of it revived me, and with a massive effort, I stuck my arm out and grabbed it. I tipped my head back and let the blood wash down my throat, feeling like a man lost in the desert who's just happened upon a fully functioning water park with poolside bar.

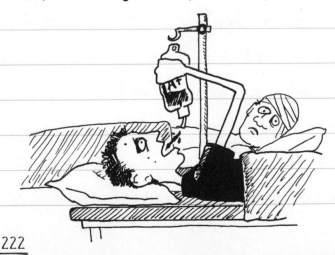

The blood was type A+, which is my least favorite flavor, but right then it seemed like the most delicious thing I'd ever tasted. As it flowed around my body, I slowly came back to life. At first my legs had pins and needles, and I was scared to walk in case I collapsed. But soon I could feel my feet again, and I made my way down the corridor as casually as I could, though my jerky movements made me resemble the silent-movie vampire Nosferatu. I wonder if he was supposed to be suffering from blood deprivation too. It's quite a clever performance when you think about it.

A nurse asked if she could help, but I ducked away, dragging myself out the front door and down the road. It was only when I caught a reflection of myself in a shop window that I understood why she was so alarmed. I'd guzzled the blood so greedily that it had run down my chin and neck. I must have looked like a critically ill car-crash victim who was popping out for a stroll.

10:00 p.m.
I'm now waiting for the late train back to Stockfield. It's with a heavy heart that I abandon my first attempt at independence. I considered trying to survive on hospital blood bags until I found a new coven, but I had to admit that I get a pretty good deal at home.

TUESDAY, NOVEMBER 15
6:00 a.m.
By the time I got home, it was past midnight. I expected my family to be sick with worry and frantically telegraphing the Vampire Council for

help. Instead, they were all in the living room playing Scrabble, and rather than breaking into grateful tears when I returned, they casually greeted me without even pausing their game.

I asked Dad if he'd been worried about me, and he said he'd presumed I was staying with my girlfriend. This was wrong on so many levels that I could hardly count them. For a start, how can he be so oblivious to the emotional problems I've been going through recently? And even if he thought I was at Chloe's house, wouldn't he bother to check? As for my farewell note, I noticed that my caring family had used the back to jot down Scrabble scores without even bothering to read it.

On a more positive note, I've got my room back, as Auntie Ivana has been kicked out. Apparently, she started reminiscing about the days when male vampires were allowed multiple wives and then she draped her arms around Dad in a provocative way, but Mum saw it and hissed at her! Why does all the juicy stuff always happen when I'm away?

1:00 p.m.

I stayed home from school to recover from my ordeal, which Mum and Dad still haven't asked about. I appreciate they've got their own problems, what with Grandpa inviting every vampire under the moon to stay with us, but you'd think they'd notice when their most important child goes missing.

The good news is that I've beendrinking lots

of thick type B+ blood and I'm feeling much better. I considered stringing out my illness to get the rest of the week off school, but I can't bear lying in bed and listening to Grandpa humming funeral dirges to himself, so I'm going back tomorrow.

WEDNESDAY, NOVEMBER 16

Once again, I'm behind on the juicy gossip. I went back to school today and found out that Jason has dumped Chloe! Obviously, I've moved on with my life and have no personal interest, but it's still quite a dramatic turn of events.

I saw Jason hanging around with the tough gang at lunch, but I couldn't see Chloe anywhere. It was probably just as well, as I'd have been unable to resist reminding her how I'd warned her about the flea-ridden cur.

THURSDAY, NOVEMBER 17

I was looking around for Chloe at lunch today when I saw the Goths sitting on the steps behind the gym. But the weird thing was, they weren't dressed as Goths anymore. They'd replaced their long coats with regulation school blazers, and they'd all returned their dyed-black hair to their natural colors (bright red in Si's case).

I was curious to find out how the principal had managed to reel in these notorious rebels, so I went over for a chat. As soon as Brian saw me approaching, he asked if I'd heard the good news. I said I already knew about Chloe getting dumped and it was neither good nor bad news as far as I was concerned. But then he said he'd been referring to the good news about Jesus.

John smiled and produced a crucifix from his backpack, and I collapsed to the ground in agony. It turns out that the Goths have all found God since I last spoke to them. Apparently, they were hanging around the graveyard one Sunday when a man convinced them to come to his evangelical church, and they all saw the light. They've changed the name of their band from Feast of the Devil to Feast of the Ascension, and they've already got a tour of churches lined up. Brian said turning into a Christian rock band was fairly straightforward, as they just had to change the word "Satan" to "God" in their songs and turn their upside-down crosses the right way up.

Well, good luck to them. It's up to them what they believe. I just can't go near them ever again without getting a migraine.

FRIDAY, NOVEMBER 18

I was reading in the library at lunch when Chloe sat down next to me. At first I was angry with her for assuming I'd come running back as soon as her stupid werewolf dumped her, but she looked upset, so I didn't say anything. Plus, sitting next to her in the library reminded me of better times earlier this year. It's amazing to think that it was only a few short months ago that I was sitting there trying to pluck up the courage to ask her out.

I asked Chloe if she was upset about getting dumped. She said it was fine because she didn't fancy him anymore anyway. It took more willpower for me to resist saying "I told you so" than it ever did to hold off from drinking her blood.

SATURDAY, NOVEMBER 19

I've been wondering if I should take Chloe back if she asks me out again. I know it's pathetic to accept someone back when they've dumped you, but by refusing to transform her, I effectively broke up with her. I wonder if things would have been simpler if I'd agreed to turn her when she asked. If nothing else, I'd have been able to keep my vampire powers and I could be dishing out humiliating defeat to

Jason on Wednesday afternoons rather than sitting on my own in the library.

SUNDAY, NOVEMBER 20

My sister was sent to her room today for announcing that she's converted to Buddhism! I can't believe she hasn't figured out yet that religions make us feel sick. She's been a vampire for eighty-five years!

She came downstairs in tears a couple of hours later, claiming that she didn't know Buddhism was a religion and that she was just copying her friend Kanishka. My parents sent her straight back upstairs, and quite rightly. I don't care if it was a mistake. She needs to stop copying her friends. If Kanishka told her to stick her hand in a font of holy water, would she do that, too?

MONDAY, NOVEMBER 21
2:00 p.m.

Breaking gossip: Jason has a new girlfriend already! He's started going out with Jacqui less than a week after breaking up with Chloe. Harsh.

Chloe sat next to me at lunch again. I bet she wants me to go out with her once more to get revenge, but I'm not going to let her use me. If I do accept her back, I'll be sure to check she isn't doing it just to spite Jason.

8:00 p.m.

Love is so confusing. I don't want this emotional roller coaster. I just want a quiet life. Or the closest thing to a quiet life that a blood-drinking fiend can reasonably expect.

TUESDAY, NOVEMBER 22

Chloe sat next to me in math today, which caused some excitement among the class gossips. Fine, let them talk, there's nothing going on. It did feel sort of right, though, so I think I will accept when she asks me out again.

WEDNESDAY, NOVEMBER 23

Tonight I asked Grandpa what he used to do when girls begged him to transform them. I was expecting him to spout some ancient rules, but he just said he made sure they didn't have his real phone number and let out a dirty cackle. Then he boasted about how he's had more human girlfriends than I've had hot blood.

THURSDAY, NOVEMBER 24
1:00 p.m.

Chloe is sitting opposite me as I write these words. She still hasn't worked up the courage to ask me out. I expect she's worried she'll be overpowered by the urge to become a vampire again. Well, she

need worry no more, because I've made a decision. When she asks me out again, not only will I accept, but I'll also transform her. All she has to do is make the first move.

6:00 p.m.

My sister came home in tears this afternoon because she went round to her friend Lucy's house to see some new kittens and they attacked her. Not that a litter of newborn kittens can do much damage to a vampire. From what I could gather, they did little but climb on her and clasp their tiny gums on her.

It seems she deliberately neglected to mention these animals when she told Mum and Dad she was going to see Lucy, knowing full well they'd forbid the visit. I can't understand why she won't get it into her dense skull that all animals hate us. Every other vampire manages to hate them in return, but she just has to be different.

FRIDAY, NOVEMBER 25

Chloe still hasn't asked me out, so I'm going to

have to tell her about my decision to accept her back. Obviously, I couldn't raise such a sensitive topic in school, so I've arranged to meet her in the graveyard at nine o'clock tomorrow night. In the moonlit cemetery I'll reveal that I'm now fully prepared to go out with her again and turn her into a vampire. Just think of all the heartache I could have avoided if I'd done that in the first place!

SATURDAY, NOVEMBER 26

I spent most of today getting my outfit ready for tonight. I've decided to go for one of Dad's velvet suits. I'm sure that wearing all this garb in a graveyard will make me look like a cheesy vampire from Scooby-Doo or something, but Chloe loves all that stuff, so it could be just the thing to rekindle our romance. I confidently predict that by the time I write my next diary entry, I'll have transformed Chloe and sorted out my complicated love life once and for all.

SUNDAY, NOVEMBER 27

I think it's time I got some of last night's events down on paper. Perhaps doing so will help me come to terms with them.

I waited in the graveyard at nine, but there was no sign of Chloe. I didn't want to give up and go home, as I knew it would be hard for her to slip away from her parents. Plus, it's not like I had anything else to do.

Just after midnight I heard a rustling from behind a gravestone. At first I was too frightened to investigate, but then I told myself it was ridiculous for a vampire to be so cowardly, even in a graveyard at night.

Something was hiding behind one of the stones. As I stepped toward it, the clouds parted to reveal a full moon, and I realized I'd made a terrible mistake.

I tried to turn back, but it was too late. A huge werewolf lumbered out and pinned me to the ground. I thrashed my head around to avoid its stinky drool as it snapped at my neck with its yellow teeth. Eventually, I managed to get a hand around its muzzle and wrestle it off. I gave it a firm kick in the flank, which sent it yelping out of the graveyard.

I didn't know if Jason had found out about my meeting with Chloe and had deliberately chosen to gate-crash it in wolf form or if I'd bumped into him on the wrong night by accident, but I did know that he'd brutally attacked me. Rather than feeling scared, as I'd been the first time I'd seen him as a wolf, I was overwhelmed with anger. All the hatred I'd ever felt for him welled up inside me, and I ran after him to finish what he'd started.

I chased the Jason wolf down the deserted streets toward Stockfield Moor. At first he was just a dark blur in the distance, but before long, I gained on him. It was only when I overtook a car that I realized I was running at full vampire speed again for the first time since that hairy fiend had stolen my girlfriend.

Not that I had much time to ponder this. I was driven by my desire to attack as the last of the suburbs turned to open fields, and I pursued Jason across dark moorland. So this was it. I was about to fight a werewolf to the death, just as Dad's crusty old book said I should have done the moment I discovered its existence.

I finally caught up with the Jason wolf on the edge of a wood below Stockfield Moor. I grabbed him by the throat, summoning all my strength to snap his neck, but he was covered in slippery mud and wriggled free.

The wolf retreated toward the wood and became harder to see in the fading moonlight. From what I could tell, Jason was turning back into human form, with his jaws shrinking back into his face. I kept up the chase, figuring that I could still give him a good beating even if he was human again, but when the creature glanced back at me from the edge of the wood, I saw something that made me stop in my tracks. The werewolf wasn't Jason at all. It was Chloe.

MONDAY, NOVEMBER 28

First things first. I have my vampire powers back now. I returned to Stockfield Moor this morning, and I can confirm that I can now set off my super-natural speed and strength as easily as before.

As for what's going on with the town's werewolf population, I'm not entirely sure. Chloe wasn't in school today. I stopped by her house, but her mum told me she was ill. As I was walking away, I saw Chloe's pale face appear at her bedroom window. I did a phone mime to see if she wanted to call me, but she shook her head.

As far as I can work out from my calendar, she'll have one more transformation tonight, and then she'll be human again until next month. I just hope she doesn't come round here to snack on me. I'd better double-lock the front door to be on the safe side.

TUESDAY, NOVEMBER 29

I feel strangely relaxed about the whole business now. Or, at least, as relaxed as an undead being who's just found out that his ex-girlfriend is a wolf is ever likely to feel.

I was on my way to school this morning when Chloe texted to ask me to meet her in the graveyard. I was shocked that someone who was so recently a class officer was suggesting truancy, but I expect changing species will do that to you.

Chloe was waiting for me right near the spot where she attacked me on Saturday. I pointed this out, and she said she didn't remember a thing. I told her I'd have taken a picture if she hadn't been trying to kill me, but it failed to raise a smile.

She said she'd come to meet me on Saturday night just as we'd agreed. But as she approached the graveyard, a full moon appeared and she felt an unbearable itching all over her body and looked on in horror as her limbs swelled. She remembered trying to call for help but heard nothing but a deep howl. After that, she had a dream about flying horizontally along the ground, and her next clear memory was of dashing for cover in the woods.

It was in those woods, freezing, naked, and covered in mud, that she began to understand

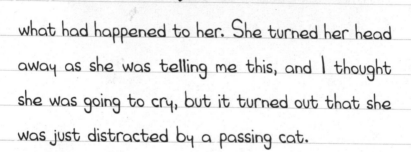

what had happened to her. She turned her head away as she was telling me this, and I thought she was going to cry, but it turned out that she was just distracted by a passing cat.

I said I felt partly responsible for the tragic turn of events and apologized for refusing to turn her into a vampire when she asked. But before I could elaborate, she interrupted me. She said that being a wolf was brilliant, and my view of it as some kind of misfortune was typical of vampire arrogance. I told her I was just trying to be nice and there was no need to bite my hand off, like I was a mailman or something.

Chloe then stormed off with typical animal irrationality. It was too late for me to go to school and too early to go back home, so I selected Chopin's "Funeral March" on my iPod and had a peaceful lie-down on a mossy grave. I really should do that more often.

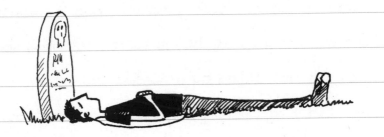

WEDNESDAY, NOVEMBER 30

Chloe was back in school today, and she apologized for her outburst yesterday. I told her it was fine and that it's natural to experience mood swings when your body changes.

Despite existing on opposite ends of the ungodly spectrum, we seem to be getting on well again. At lunch we went to the far corner of the playground, so she could tell me more about how she became a wereperson.

She said she'd asked Jason if she could watch him turn into a wolf, but he'd said it was private. She was determined to witness it and had called round at his house on the first night of the full moon last month. When she found it empty, she spent the rest of the night searching for Jason and his family, finally tracking them down to the north side of Pottsworth Moor.

She greeted the Jason wolf, expecting him to recognize her, but he pawed her aside and dashed away into the forest. She suffered a few painful scratches, but she had assumed that she'd need a full bite to catch lycanthropy.

She'd been as surprised as I was when the next full moon came round and she transformed.

She said she'd been feeling fantastic ever since her transformation. She'd discovered new sounds and smells, and she felt more alive than ever before. She said that she wished I could know what it was like. Yeah, I'm sure being a mongrel is brilliant and everything, but I'll stick to being a more upmarket creature of the night, if that's quite all right.

So we've made friends again. But before the rumors start, I want to make it clear that we're not going to become an item. According to Dad's book *Defeating the Lycanthrope Menace*, werewolves and vampires are strictly forbidden to become lovers under threat of execution by both the Vampire Council and the Werewolf Trade Union.

248

Having said that, the book does relate the story of a werewolf and a vampire in eighteenth-century Sussex who fell in love and produced an offspring called a "werepire," which was said to be the most evil creature that ever lived. By the age of eight it had already killed over three thousand people, started two wars, and invented a debt-consolidation scheme. Some say the werepire was eventually destroyed when a silver stake was rammed in its heart. Others say it survived and went on to a successful career judging TV talent shows.

THURSDAY, DECEMBER 1

Chloe sat next to me in math, and it didn't take long for my silly classmates to ask if we were going out again. Just because we're friends, they automatically assume that we're an item once more. There is such a thing as mature, platonic friendship, you know. Plus, I don't like her now that her eyebrows meet in the middle.

I have to say I'm impressed with myself for staying friends with Chloe despite her species change. Perhaps I'll go down in history as the first vampire who was progressive enough to make peace with wolfkind, and one day we'll all live together in harmony, thanks to me. Having said that, I still hate Jason. I'm prepared to tolerate intelligent werewolves like Chloe, but not stupid dogs like him.

In other news, the whiteheads on my chin have cleared up again. I wonder if this means my vampire attractiveness is coming back. I'm not sure I really want it to. I don't think I could cope with another slew of illiterate love letters right now. I might try to offset it by wearing a school blazer and getting a pudding-bowl haircut like Nick from the chess club.

FRIDAY, DECEMBER 2

Now that the shock of last weekend is wearing off, my thoughts have turned to the subject of my vampire powers. It's all rather strange. When Chloe dumped me, my powers disappeared, and I assumed I had to win her back for them to return. But then I survived a major crisis on Saturday night, and they returned by themselves.

I can't put my finger on it, but I think my powers appear whenever I truly feel like a vampire, but they desert me whenever I feel like a boring old human. So when I'm racing across moonlit moors in pursuit of werewolves, I can access my powers; but when I'm moping around feeling sorry for myself, I can't. I think that whether I'm single or not, I'll always be able to access my powers—as long as I believe I'm worthy of being a vampire.

SATURDAY, DECEMBER 3

I went out to Pottsworth Moor with Chloe today to test her werewolf speed. It's weird that she can run as fast as me now. She used to have to wait for me when I sprinted off, but it's much more fun now that we can race. She also has amazing strength, though to be honest, I can't see any evidence that werewolves develop supernatural beauty. If anything, she was prettier as a human. I guess that makes sense, as werewolves don't need beauty to attract their prey like we do. Their seduction of prey doesn't get much more sophisticated than jumping on it and chomping off its limbs.

In addition to her strength and speed, Chloe has developed other powers since her change. She has an amazing sense of smell and can follow scents over great distances with stunning accuracy. Her hearing is also incredibly sensitive, and she keeps telling me I don't need to shout (I have advised her never to see the group Mask of Sanity live in concert). Also, she is unable to resist running after a stick if I throw it. I admit that I tested this last characteristic several times, but I must stress that I did this in the interests of paranormal research and not because I found it incredibly funny.

SUNDAY, DECEMBER 4

3:00 p.m.

I went round to Chloe's house this morning with Dad's copy of *Defeating the Lycanthrope Menace*. He'd go nuts if he knew I'd taken it out of his study without asking him, but judging by the amount of dust on it, he hasn't opened it for over a century.

I read aloud some passages from the book, making sure to translate its prejudiced tone into a more neutral one. I told her that werewolves could be killed by silver bullets, leaving out the book's section of handy hints on where to buy them. I outlined the ancient feud between vampires and werewolves and told her not to be offended if I didn't invite her round for dinner anytime soon. She said she didn't like my mum's cooking anyway, so I said I didn't know dog meat needed heating up. She smiled at my joke, so I think she must be feeling more relaxed about her condition now.

She seemed downcast when I told her that if werewolves avoid silver bullets, they can live for 150 years. I think she'd assumed they were immortal like us. Still, 150 years isn't bad. It's twice as long as the average human gets. And I bet she'll be glad she's not immortal by the time she's in her late 140s.

I wonder how old Jason's parents are. They could be in their nineties, I suppose, which might explain why they love corned beef so much. They ought to be richer by now, though. They could have bought a house for about £500 in the thirties that would be worth a quarter of a million now. Instead, they're stuck in Stockfield's worst neighborhood. That's what happens when you squander your money on processed meat.

In the afternoon I took Dad's book home and left Chloe to catch up with her homework. I think she's started to worry about her schoolwork now that it's sunk in that she's not immortal. It's all well and good for me to coast along, as I'll get another chance to learn it all again soon. But she'll grow older eventually, so she'll need a good degree and a well-paying job if she's going to keep herself in flea collars and bones. Plus, she'll have three fewer days this month to study for her exams. There's no point trying to memorize the periodic table when your IQ has dropped to single digits.

1:00 a.m.

I went for a run on Pottsworth Moor with Chloe tonight. It was raining heavily, so we figured we could get away with unleashing our powers without anyone noticing. Unfortunately, we got a bit carried away and ran all the way back at top speed. As we arrived outside my house, I saw Grandpa looking out of his window and tutting.

Although he hasn't said anything yet, I'm terrified he'll work out that Chloe's a werewolf, and Mum and Dad will make me battle her to the death for the sake of stupid tradition. I don't want to murder my ex-girlfriend. I'm just not the type.

MONDAY, DECEMBER 5

Mum and Dad were out hunting tonight, so Grandpa came up to my room to have a word. I pretended to be on my phone to avoid talking to him, but he went right ahead and lectured me anyway. He probably doesn't even know what a cell phone is.

Grandpa said he knew what I'd been up to with Chloe. I was anticipating a windy speech about how lycanthropes are dangerous and how I'm bringing our coven into disrepute by consorting with them. But luckily for me, the old fool had got the wrong end of the stick entirely.

He said he'd worked out from the speed Chloe was running that I'd transformed her into a vampire. He said that it was irresponsible to avoid telling my parents I'd created a new vampire and that if I didn't tell them soon, he would.

258

Although I was relieved he hadn't figured out that things were far more serious, I was still angry with him for meddling. I said he was right about Chloe and that I was sure my parents would be interested to find out. I said they'd also be interested to find out that he has full vampire strength and speed, and just pretends to be frail so he doesn't have to do anything.

Grandpa weighed the pleasure of ratting me out against the loss of his cushy little scam, and then a fake grin spread across his face. He said that vampires will be vampires and he'd done much worse in his day, so we should forget about it. Then he patted my head and winked as if he'd acted out of kindness rather than fear of actually having to lift a finger for once in his death.

TUESDAY, DECEMBER 6

I went to the bowling alley with Chloe tonight, but we both scored a strike every time, so it soon got boring. We gave up and went out to Stockfield Moor and invented our own game, where we had to throw a large boulder off a hill and see how far we could make it roll. It was much more enjoyable than bowling, and we didn't have to wear those ridiculous shoes.

I was winning for most of the evening, but Chloe had sneaked ahead by the time she threw the rock too far and crushed a Hummer, at which point we had to stop. She declared herself the winner, but I think it should have counted as a draw. It wasn't exactly worth restarting the vampire-werewolf war, though.

WEDNESDAY, DECEMBER 7

Mr. Byrne gave us a talk about "time management" instead of a normal English lesson today. He said we all had to draw a grid for next January and plan a study timetable for our practice exams, so we wouldn't get too stressed if we had two on the same day.

I enjoyed drawing the table and coloring it in with my felt-tips, although I've got no more intention of studying now than I had last time I took these exams, or the time before that.

When Mr. Byrne looked at my timetable, he said he admired my dedication, but I mustn't push myself too hard. I couldn't work out what he was going on about until I realized I'd drawn a twenty-four-hour grid and scheduled study sessions through each night. I keep forgetting that humans sleep.

THURSDAY, DECEMBER 8
6:00 p.m.

Jason turned up late for math today, and the only free chair was the one next to me. I tried to spread my books across the whole desk, as I didn't think I'd be able to focus on trigonometry with a vicious murderer next to me. It didn't stop him from taking the seat and blasting me with dog breath all through class, though.

He asked why I hadn't been at cross-country practice since that time I lost. I wanted to say that it's hard to care about such trivial things when your ex-girlfriend has been transformed into a wolf by a callous brute, but instead, I said that cross-country running wasn't a competitive sport so it wasn't possible to lose at it.

He then boasted that he'd completed the course ages before everyone else every time and that Mr. Moss had said he was the greatest cross-country runner the school had ever known. I said that the school was only founded in 1984, so it wasn't such a big deal. At the end of the lesson he said he might see me at cross-country next week.

Although I might be crediting him with more subtlety than he's capable of, I think Jason was laying down a challenge. Fine, I'll return to the running club on Wednesday. Now that I've got my vampire speed back, it's that mangy mutt who should be worried.

10:00 p.m.

Tonight I heard my parents telling my sister off for playing basketball too well. Apparently, she scored twenty-five points in her last PE class and came home with her backpack stuffed with leaflets about national tournaments, so Dad has grounded her.

I suppose I should try to hold back in the race on Wednesday, in case they find out and I get the same punishment. On the other hand, imagine the look on Jason's smug potato face if I turn my vampire speed up to maximum and leave him floundering. Is that worth getting grounded?

Yes, I think it is.

FRIDAY, DECEMBER 9

Mr. Byrne let us do a Secret Santa today. He put everyone's name into a hat, and we all had to

draw someone out and buy them a present for a pound. I drew Darren, but then Craig drew Jason, and he let me trade with him for fifty pence.

I thought about buying Jason some wolfsbane, a flower that's considered harmful to werewolves. But I couldn't find any at the florist's, and if it turned out to be a myth, it would look like I'd bought him some flowers and Craig would tease me. Instead, I went to the pet shop and bought Jason a squeaky toy bone. It's hardly subtle, but you need to match jokes to the comprehension level of your audience.

I hope Jason didn't pick my name. His idea of a present is probably a dead bird he's dragged in from the garden.

SATURDAY, DECEMBER 10

I went out to Pottsworth Moor today to race against Chloe as practice for my showdown with Jason on Wednesday. As far as I can tell, vampire top speed and werewolf top speed are pretty much the same, so even if I completely go for it, there's no guarantee I'll beat him.

I really need to win, though. This will be the last outing of the cross-country running club, so I won't get another chance to triumph over Jason.

Chloe asked if she could join in the race too,

and I gave her a lecture about how you need to keep your powers under wraps if you don't want to end up in the Natural History Museum. It was entirely hypocritical of me to go on like that, but she's newer to the supernatural realm and needs to be more careful. Do as I say, not as I do, as Dad says.

To underline my point, I set a sensible human pace for us to jog home, although it wasn't long before Chloe got too excited and chased after a car.

SUNDAY, DECEMBER 11

Mum wants us all to stay with some vampires in Edinburgh for a few days after Christmas. She said it would be nice for us to go away together like a normal family. I hate her fixation with being a "normal family." We're not a normal family; we're bloodsucking freaks, and no amount of pretending to drink coffee at highway rest stops is going to alter that.

I told her that I have my practice tests in January and need to stay at home to study. She tried to convince me to go with them, but after all the hassle she's given me over the years about concentrating on my schoolwork, she could hardly insist.

She said it would be nice for me to meet some other vampires for a change, and I might even make some new friends. I told her that if Grandpa and Ivana are anything to go by, other vampires are all lazy freeloaders who expect others to fetch blood for them and I would have nothing in common with them. She said it sounded like I'd have plenty in common with them, so I said I wished she'd never transformed me and slammed the door.

MONDAY, DECEMBER 12

I absolutely give up on this ridiculous species. Today I finally received a reply from the publisher. I've glued the letter directly into my diary, as it's so staggeringly imbecilic that any attempt to summarize its contents would make my brain leak out through my ears.

Dear Nigel,

Many thanks for submitting your novel, *Dark Embrace of the Night*, to us. Unfortunately, it's not the sort of thing we're looking for at the moment. We felt that much of the plot was

269

cliched, and the characters lacked dimension. Also, at little more than 3,000 words, it isn't long enough to be a novel. You will need to write at least twenty times that amount, I'm afraid!

Furthermore, you might have noticed that vampires are very much in vogue at the moment, so there's no shortage of these manuscripts doing the rounds. A word to the wise: One of our junior editors has heard that shape-shifting manticores will be the next big thing. Perhaps an idea for your next project?

Thank you once again for your submission, and sorry it wasn't right for us.

Yours sincerely,

Xander De Pfeffel, MA (Cantab)

Senior Editor

I have no idea what "shape-shifting manticores" are, and I can't even be bothered Googling them. Oh well, it's their loss. I gave these fools the chance to publish a work of genuine supernatural power, and they threw it away. Hear that, Mr. De Pfeffel Cantab or whatever your name is? That's the sound of the villa in the South of France you could have bought crumbling to dust.

TUESDAY, DECEMBER 13

Mr. Byrne gave out the Secret Santa presents today, and the look on Jason's face when he opened his was priceless. I tried really hard not to laugh when he gave me a dirty look. Oh yeah, want to make something of it, Scrappy-Doo?

Someone unoriginal bought me some constipation tablets, which raised a few idiotic titters. Yeah, like that joke isn't three months out-of-date.

Now I'm lying in bed and conserving my energy for the race tomorrow. I don't want to wait twelve more hours to beat him. I want to do it now.

Time to school this fool.

WEDNESDAY, DECEMBER 14

I couldn't concentrate in school today because I kept glancing at Jason's spud face and feeling angry that such a pitiful example of an inferior species could ever beat me at anything.

When at last the time came for the cross-country club to assemble, Jason sat behind me on the minibus and kept shoving his knees into the back of my seat to annoy me.

The minibus pulled into the Pottsworth Moor parking lot, and I somehow resisted the temptation to turn round to Jason and shout, "Walkies!" As soon as we got out of the bus, we both dashed straight off, ignoring Mr. Moss's request that we join in with his stupid warming-up exercises. We both kept a restrained pace while the others could still see us, and we were tied as we approached the first bend in the path.

But the minute we were out of sight of the others, we both stepped up to the pace of a good human athlete. I was reluctant to use my full vampire powers in front of Jason. I reasoned that while he might have worked out that there was something unusual about me from previous PE classes, the chances of him concluding anything beyond that were slim. If I went to full speed, there would be no denying that I was a supernatural, and there could be all sorts of repercussions. He'd tell his parents, they'd find my parents, the ancient war between our peoples would flare up again, my PlayStation would get broken, and so on.

Jason soon made the decision for me by zooming off ahead. I couldn't exactly let him get away with it, could I? I unleashed my full vampire speed and flew down the path until I caught up with him.

I pushed my body as fast as it could go, and then I looked across in disbelief as Jason pulled ahead once again. I had to face the horrible possibility that when both are running at maximum speed, a male werewolf has the edge on a male vampire. I made a solemn note to revise my letter to the manufacturer of Top Trumps.

I summoned up my last reserves of energy and gained slightly on Jason, but it wasn't enough. We were rapidly approaching the end of the course, and I could go no faster. I was seconds away from letting down my entire species. But as we approached the last corner, I had an idea. Leaping into the air, I snapped a branch from an overhanging tree, called out Jason's name, and threw it away from the path.

Forgetting the race and his rivalry with me, Jason ran after the stick, leaving me to jog to the end of the course at a normal human pace.

So that was it. I won the race, and Jason trundled over a couple of minutes later, red-faced with anger, with the stick still clasped in his mouth. Didn't like that, did you, little doggie?

THURSDAY, DECEMBER 15

While I'm still proud of my victory yesterday, I'm worried that it came at too great a cost.

When Jason passed me in the corridor this afternoon, he said he knew I was one of the "cold ones." Quick as a flash, I said I knew he was one of the hairy ones. He said at least he was alive. This comment was so below the belt that the only comeback I could think of was to repeat it in a sarcastic voice. I admit that this was nowhere near my usual standard, but it was the best I could do under the pressure of the moment.

I should have known that using my full speed in front of Jason would have serious consequences. I just hope it hasn't awoken the ancient and deadly animosity between our races that will lead to a mass uprising of the armies of the night and envelop the world in darkness. That's not going to look good on my end-of-year report card.

FRIDAY, DECEMBER 16
11:00 a.m.

Today was the last day of class before Christmas, so we were all allowed to bring in games. I brought Connect Four, as I've played it so much that I know how to counter every possible move, and it's mathematically impossible to beat me.

When Jason walked past my desk, I asked him if he wanted to play a game, adding that it wasn't as hard as cross-country running. This must have struck a nerve, as he knocked all the pieces to the floor and told me to pick them up. Great retort, Jason, must have taken you ages to come up with that.

I counted to ten to stop myself feeling angry, but Jason repeated the numbers in the style of the Count from Sesame Street, which didn't help. I reminded myself how serious a showdown between our peoples would be, and I calmly picked the red and yellow counters from the floor.

I laid the pieces out on the table again. Jason swept them back down to the ground, and this time I found it harder to turn the other cheek. Craig tried to stir things up by asking me what I was going to do. I said I didn't need to do anything because Jason's bark was worse than his bite.

I now realize it was very provocative of me to use this kind of wolfist language. Jason launched himself at me as if I were an intruder in his garden. I struggled to hold him back, but he still managed to land a firm whack to the side of my head. Obviously, as a vampire, I don't feel pain, but it's still annoying when your skull gets bashed around like that.

I wanted to set off my vampire strength

and fling the brute out of the window, but the entire class had now gathered around, and several of them were filming it on their phones. If the ancient rivalry between lycanthrope and Nosferatu is to be reawakened, let's at least try to keep it off YouTube.

I summoned up enough strength to slam Jason across the floor of the classroom. He was running back to me on all fours when Mr. Wilson dashed into the room and broke up the fight.

I bet Mr. Wilson doesn't know how brave he was. He could be the first human to break up a vampire-werewolf battle since the nineteenth-century paranormal investigator Digby Kronos. And he was armed with a case full of wooden stakes, silver bullets, and holy water, rather than just a chalkboard eraser.

Mr. Wilson then told us to wait outside the principal's office, which is where I'm writing this now, with Jason glaring at me. I'm a bit worried about what he might do. I know he took design and technology as his electives. I just hope he hasn't learned how to make wooden stakes yet.

8:00 p.m.

At first the principal threatened to call our parents to collect us. I wanted to tell him that he had no idea of the forces he was unleashing.

If our parents met face-to-face, all manner of supernatural fury would break loose. Was that something he wanted so soon after the science labs had been refurbished?

In the end I managed to avoid war by apologizing to Jason. He said sorry to me too, and we were sent to sit in the corridor until the end of the day.

I told Jason that I'd seen him transform with his family on the night of the full moon, but I hadn't told anyone because I didn't want to rock the boat. He mulled this over for a couple of minutes before admitting that I'd probably done the right thing. He said we should keep our mouths shut to avoid our families ripping each other to pieces. I was about to say that we should let sleeping dogs lie, but I thought this might also count as an offensive turn of phrase.

When the principal called us back at the end of the day, we told him we'd made up. He said he'd put it down to high spirits on the last day of class and keep it off our permanent records.

As we walked home together, we had an interesting chat about our families. Jason asked me if it was true that we killed humans. I said that it didn't happen as often as everyone thinks, as they can recover if we don't drain too much of their blood.

He said it was also rare for his family to kill. They always bring plenty of raw meat along on full moons so they can feed as soon as they transform and avoid the hunger that drives them to murder. He said that sometimes a human gets in the way by mistake and gets killed or turned into a wolf, but thankfully, this hadn't happened for a long time. I was dying to tell him about Chloe, but I kept it zipped. It's up to her whether she wants to reveal herself to Jason's pack.

Just as Jason was turning off onto his street, I asked him whether it was my supernatural speed or beauty that had made him realize I was a vampire. He said it was the night he'd spotted me reading *Dracula* and drinking blood in a graveyard.

Perhaps Jason isn't as stupid as I thought.

SATURDAY, DECEMBER 17

The Christmas holidays begin today, which should give me a rest after all the hassle of the last few weeks.

Although Christmas is traditionally a time of feasting and merriment for humans, it's a

284

terrible time for us. This is because humans drink so much alcohol over the festive period that their blood makes us ill, so we have to spend the whole time unfreezing thermoses of safe blood in the microwave. They never taste as good as the fresh stuff, even if you use a delicious flavor like AB+.

Also, Mum and Dad refuse to buy me presents because we don't celebrate Christmas. So what? Sanjay's parents are Hindus, and he got an Xbox 360 last year.

I went round to see Chloe this evening. She'd heard about my fight with Jason and was all set to lecture me about controlling my temper, but I told her we'd made friends and she was very relieved. I said I was glad we'd avoided a war so my posse wouldn't have to pop a silver cap in her, and I did some gangsta hand gestures for a joke. She said she was glad she didn't have to waste any wooden stakes on my heart that could be used for a perfectly good garden fence.

SUNDAY, DECEMBER 18

I called Chloe for a chat this evening, but she seemed quieter than usual, so I asked her if the novelty of being a werewolf was wearing off. She said it wasn't, but she was very worried about what would happen during the next full moon. I have to admit that I'd been so busy congratulating myself about extending the hand of friendship to wolfkind that I hadn't considered this.

Although she's perfectly civil to me now, the animal part of her brain will take over when  the next full moon comes around, and she'll rip my head off as soon as look at me. Even if she only chewed off a limb, I might never see it again.*

*Having said that, Dad's book mentions a battle where a werewolf swallowed the hand of a vampire, only to look on in shock as the hand ripped its way out of its stomach and fixed itself back on the vampire's body, causing great discomfort and embarrassment to all.

MONDAY, DECEMBER 19

Some carol singers called round this evening, and my sister foolishly opened the door. Like anything to do with religion, Christmas carols cause us great distress, which is why we're not supposed to answer the door at this time of year. Unfortunately, some members of our family are too dense to remember simple instructions like that.

As soon as my sister swung the door open, the singers launched into "Away in a Manger," causing us all to jam our fingers into our ears and scream in agony. When they finished, Dad gave them twenty pounds on the condition that they never return. They seemed taken aback by this reaction, but I had no sympathy. I don't go round to their houses and run my fingernails down a blackboard until they give me money.

TUESDAY, DECEMBER 20
6:00 p.m.

Chloe is still fretting about her next transformation. She's calculated it will take place on
Boxing Day, when she's supposed to be staying
with relatives. The last thing she wants is to
come round on the morning of the 27th with the
shredded remains of Auntie Joyce and Uncle
Phil in her mouth.

I offered to let her stay with me and pretend
we're studying for our exams, as the rest of my
family will be in Edinburgh then. She agreed, and
I instantly began to regret my generous offer.
I was looking forward to a quiet break, and now
I'll have to spend the whole time shouting at
her to get down off the couch.

10:00 p.m.

You'd think that after the torture the carolers put us through yesterday, my sister would have finally got the message that religious things make us ill. But that would be to assume that you were dealing with a rational being. This evening she threw a tantrum because Mum and Dad wouldn't let her take part in the school nativity play. She said that it wouldn't affect her because she didn't feel ill when they did *Grease*. Like that's the same thing! We're talking about a dramatization of the life of Christ, not a piece of fluff about an American high school. As soon as they mentioned the baby Jesus, she'd be rolling around on the floor and projectile vomiting. It would be more like a school production of *The Exorcist* than the nativity story.

290

WEDNESDAY, DECEMBER 21

I've come up with a great plan to keep Chloe safe during her next transformation: I'm going to lock her in the basement!

I went out this afternoon to buy four combination locks, which I'll use to fix Chloe's arms and legs to the pipes in the basement. I can then leave her howling safely away for each night of her transformation. And here's the crafty bit: Every night I'll write the combinations to the locks on the floor in chalk so she can read them when she's human again, key the numbers in with the tips of her fingers, clean up, and get dressed with her dignity intact.

I invited Chloe round this evening to show her the setup, and she seemed impressed. She's still nervous about turning into a wolf again, but at least she knows she isn't going to bite anyone this time. As a liberal and a regular supporter of charities, she was having a moral crisis about eating strangers.

THURSDAY, DECEMBER 22

My iPod fell out of my pocket in the shopping center today, and I couldn't find it anywhere. In the end I had to call Chloe and get her to track its scent. It turns out that someone had handed it in at the lost and found office of the bus station. Though I'm a sworn enemy of all wolfkind, I have to admit they have some useful skills. If I'd lost that iPod, I'd have to use my really old one that you can only fit twenty thousand songs on.

After that, we sat at a table outside Starbucks and looked at all the shallow humans darting around with their bags full of consumer goods they don't need. I sipped a thermos of type A- while Chloe ate a pungent can of corned beef.

She's still worried about her upcoming transformations. I'm sure she'll get used to them as she settles into wolf life, but this will be only her second lot. I remember being very upset and confused the first time my fangs extended, but I soon learned to live with it.

I asked her if changing hurts, and she said it hurts more than I could possibly imagine. That wouldn't be hard. Although I get headaches when I smell garlic or look at religious stuff, I haven't felt proper physical pain since I was a human eighty-five years ago. I do get a sort of tingle when my fangs extend, though. It must be weird when every single bone in your body grows at once.

FRIDAY, DECEMBER 23

My family invited me to play charades with them this evening, but I soon bailed out because they insisted on choosing books that were popular ages before I was born. Every time they mimed a book title, I knew it would be something I'd never heard of. They groaned at me for failing to guess *The Castle of Otrantro*, *The History of Caliph Vathek*, and *The Mysteries of Udolpho*, yet when my sister mimed *High School Musical* and I got it right, they said it didn't count because it was too obscure!

I told them I was happy to play board games with printed instructions that we could agree on before playing, but I would no longer join in any game in which they could change the rules to suit themselves.

SATURDAY, DECEMBER 24
4:00 p.m.

We were invited to a Christmas party by our neighbors, the Pattersons, this afternoon. I presumed Mum would get us out of it, but I was forgetting her silly obsession with us being a normal family, so we all had to go and stand in the corner of their living room. I know I complain about my parents occasionally, but I'm glad I don't have to live with any of those humans. They just stood around sipping eggnog and talking about house prices. I felt like attacking one of them just to liven things up.

Although Mrs. Patterson was able to accept that none of us wanted a drink, she wouldn't let us get away without trying the mince pies. We all had to take one and pretend to eat it while really stuffing it down the radiator. Eventually, pie filling began to leak out of the bottom and Mr. Patterson called a plumber. We decided to leave before he turned up and revealed that ungrateful guests rather than faulty valves were the problem.

As we left, Grandpa slipped some type A- into the punch from his hip thermos. I expect all those humans would have been grossed out if they knew they were drinking blood, but I don't particularly care. They tried to force those disgusting mince pies on us, so it's only fair.

10:00 p.m.

My sister is looking out of the window for Santa's sleigh tonight. I can't believe she still thinks all that nonsense is real. I've tried to explain to her that it's just a story, but she's still convinced that there really is someone up there delivering wooden toys to children who didn't vandalize any bus stops this year.

Mind you, I didn't believe werewolves were real until a couple of months ago. For all I know, Santa could be real too. If he is, I'd advise him to stay away from our chimney. We're all

getting really sick of frozen blood, and some fresh stuff from a plump old man and some red-nosed reindeers would be a real treat right now.

SUNDAY, DECEMBER 25

Merry Christmas, I don't think.

I can't understand why humans spend so much of their year looking forward to this day. It doesn't seem very exciting to me.

Mum and Dad are getting into the festive spirit, though. It's only three in the afternoon and they're already on their third bottle of type AB+. Mum will be dancing on the table by five and tearfully reminiscing about the Victorian era by seven, I guarantee. Happens every year.

I think I'll go downstairs and warn Dad against drinking so much blood that he gets hung over and can't travel to Scotland tomorrow. I don't care if they miss their stupid holiday, but I don't have a backup plan for Chloe's transformation. We could try the Motor Inn near the business area, I suppose. But we'd be sure to get kicked out if she shredded the room on the first night.

MONDAY, DECEMBER 26
5:00 p.m.

Thankfully, Dad heeded my warning about over-doing it on the blood, and they all piled into the Volvo early this morning for the drive up to

Edinburgh. It's quite a distance, and Dad will
have to drive very carefully if he doesn't want
a police officer to stop him for a breath test.
You only need a tiny drop of alcohol in the blood
you've been drinking to fail one of those things
these days.

I'm so glad I got out of their little excursion.
The last time I had to sit next to my sister on
a long journey, she kicked me so hard, I fell out
of the door and into the fast lane and I nearly
got run over by a bus. If I'd been squashed,

it would have taken ages for my body to heal itself.

It's so lovely and quiet without those idiots around. I think I might move into a flat of my own soon. As soon as I get over my guilt about attacking humans, I'll be totally self-sufficient. I'll probably have to move to somewhere like Tokyo or L.A. to find friends who are cool enough for me, though.

In the meantime, I'm off to prepare the basement for Chloe tonight. This should be interesting.

4:00 a.m.

Well, that was all rather harrowing, but I'm pleased to say that my werewolf containment system was a success. It's all over for the night, and Chloe is asleep on the armchair opposite me as I write.

She came round at seven this evening, with a change of clothes in an overnight bag. I asked her how you know you're about to transform, and she said you get a painful itching all over, then it feels like your body is being stretched in every direction at once, and then you black out.

I thought it might be polite to wait for this itching to start, but I was worried the change would be too sudden for me to cope with, so I fixed her to the pipes in the basement at 11:00 p.m.

Shortly after midnight Chloe tearfully begged me to remove the locks. Dad's werewolf book had warned about these kinds of pleas, so I ignored them. And then it happened. Her bones twisted beneath her skin, her nose extended into a snout, and thick brown hairs pushed through the pores of her face.* Then her head lurched down and her cries turned into howls. I looked into her eyes for signs of recognition, but there was nothing. If she hadn't been fastened to the pipes, she would have torn me apart mercilessly. That time I lent her my markers would have counted for nothing.

There was no point trying to speak to wolf Chloe, so I chalked the lock combinations on the floor and came back upstairs. Her pining and howling was very loud, so I blasted a compilation of party hits from the stereo to mask the ungodly noise.

---

*According to Dad's book, the color of a human's hair will always be the color of their pelt when they turn into a werewolf. It claims the dark-haired ones are the most dangerous, as the red ones are easy to spot from a distance and the blond ones are easily confused and spend most of the time chasing their own tails and getting their heads stuck in paper bags.

At one point Chloe strained against her chains so violently that the whole house shook, and one of Mum's antique vases fell off the mantelpiece and smashed on the floor. I went up to the attic to find another one. She'll never notice.

After a couple of hours the howling stopped. Chloe came upstairs with her new clothes on and fell asleep on the chair, where she remains now. Her wrists and ankles look very sore, but other than that, she's unscathed. I've just noticed that her arms and legs are twitching. I wonder if she's dreaming about running.

TUESDAY, DECEMBER 27

Chloe slept through the morning, so I mopped up the slobber in the basement and went out to the supermarket to buy some meat.

I figured that Chloe wouldn't strain against her chains so much if she had some raw meat to keep her occupied. Luckily, the supermarket hadn't sold all their Christmas turkeys and they were reduced to three pounds each. I bought five, which I thought would be enough to keep the wolf from the door, if you'll pardon the expression.

Chloe was awake by the time I got back, and she said the meat looked nasty as I was chopping it up and flinging it into a bucket. I said she wouldn't think that when she was in Fido form, but I couldn't disagree with her. I don't know how humans can get on their high horses about us drinking blood and then casually chew on animal corpses.

We had a fun afternoon playing SingStar on the PlayStation. Chloe selected "Love Song for a Vampire," so to get my own back, I chose "Hungry Like the Wolf."

Soon the moon rose, and it was time to prepare for the next transformation. Chloe said she didn't want to ruin another perfectly good set of clothes, so I fetched one of Mum's huge ball gowns, which I reckoned was loose enough to cope with the transformation.

As I was fixing her locks, I asked Chloe what she'd done about clothes after her transformations last month. She admitted that she'd had to steal a yellow argyle sweater and a pair of gray trousers from a backyard clothesline one night. Luckily, her parents were still asleep when she got in, so she didn't have to pretend she'd been at an all-night rave for golfers.

I suppose I must have looked very strange chaining a teenage girl in an oversized ball gown to the pipes in my basement, but it's amazing how quickly you get used to stuff like that. Take it from someone who drinks human blood in toilet stalls in school at lunchs.

I watched her disturbing transformation again, wrote the lock combinations on the floor, and shoved the bucket of raw meat in front of her. She immediately shoved her muzzle right in and began to gnaw on it, so I left her to it. It seems to have done the trick, as she's howling much less tonight. I've still whacked up the stereo to be on the safe side, though.

WEDNESDAY, DECEMBER 28

Chloe turned back into a human and came upstairs early this morning. Once again, she slept through most of the day, we spent the evening on the PlayStation, she changed into her gown, I chained her up, she howled in terror, and I stuck the party hits on the stereo.

I have to admit I'm very pleased with my system for controlling werewolves. Perhaps one day my pioneering work will be acknowledged and I'll—

THURSDAY, DECEMBER 29
7:00 a.m.

It turns out that my system was much less foolproof than I'd thought. Just as I was writing the above words, Dad's car pulled into the driveway. I wasn't expecting my family to return so early, but they're about as good at organization as sunbathing, so I should have known better.

I tried to mask Chloe's howling by selecting "Who Let the Dogs Out?" on SingStar, but it didn't fool them. As soon as they got in, Mum and Dad followed the noise down to the basement. I went after them to explain that the wolf was Chloe, but this didn't stop them from hissing and bearing their fangs at her, which was hardly polite. I don't think I've ever seen them so angry before. Not even that time I changed the D to a B on my school report.

Soon Grandpa and my sister were down in the basement, and it looked as though no amount of pleading on my part could avert a violent supernatural showdown. Why do they always have to be so melodramatic?

I knew it was time for deeds and not words, so I grabbed the clothesline and tied it around Chloe's neck to create a leash. I then undid her locks and gripped the clothesline as the terrified Chloe wolf darted out of the basement, across the living room, and straight through the front window. A shard of glass broke off in my thigh

as I was dragged along, and I had to pick it out
so my skin wouldn't heal over it.

I'd like to think that if any insomniacs spotted
us, they'd have seen nothing more unusual than
a teenage boy taking his dog for a walk. They
might have wondered why the walk was taking
place at 2:00 a.m. and why the dog was eight
feet long and wearing a ball gown, but most
humans are so drunk at this time of year, they
probably wouldn't have noticed.

I'd hoped to keep up with Chloe and explain things when she turned human again, but the clothesline slipped out of my grasp just as we were approaching Stockfield Moor, so I let her go.

When I got home, my family refused to speak to me. I think it's fairly safe to say that I'm grounded.

12:00 p.m.
Got a text from Chloe this morning:

Just woke up wearing a ball gown with a clothesline tied round my neck and half a sheep hanging from my mouth. What happened?

I replied:

Yeah, messy night ;) My parents know about you now, so don't come round. Don't worry, though. I'll sort out everything and call you,
Nige V^^^^V

FRIDAY, DECEMBER 30

Mum and Dad still aren't talking to me. I saw Dad cleaning some antique pistols in the kitchen this morning, and I have a horrible feeling he's about to buy some silver bullets and restart the vampire-werewolf war. Maybe I should sneak out of town before it starts. I know it's all sort of my fault, but I really don't want to fight in a war. I bet I could write some good war poetry, though.

SATURDAY, DECEMBER 31

My parents are speaking to me again now, but they're still really angry. I was summoned to the study early this morning to find Mum, Dad, and

Grandpa scowling at me. I said I was sorry, but they clearly intended to make it as painful as possible.

Dad asked if I had any idea how serious what I'd done was, and I pretended I didn't. He said that vampires and werewolves had been enemies for centuries, and if they ever meet, instinct should force them to fight to the death.

I told them about Jason and his family, about

how Chloe had been accidentally transformed, and how I'd invented a good system for restraining wolfpeople. I went on to say that while I'd felt resentful and competitive toward Jason, I'd never felt any urge to kill him. I suggested that if the rest of vampirekind were as understanding as me, all supernatural beings could live together in harmony and the world would be a better place.

Dad didn't sympathize with my progressive views. Instead, he flew off the handle, ranting about how werewolves were untrustworthy and would think nothing of ripping a vampire's head off their shoulders. I was going to point out that we're not exactly without blame, but I thought it was best to keep quiet.

Then Mum burst into tears and asked if next time I felt like aiding a sworn enemy of our kind, could I at least refrain from ruining one of her best dresses in the process? Apparently, the ball gown was a present from some old archduke or another. I suggested that she might wear one of her million other dresses next time she attends a ball, which she never does anyway.

I was then sent out of the room so they could consider what to do next. Perhaps they'll kick me out of the coven; perhaps they'll confiscate my PlayStation. Either way, I don't think I'm going to have a very good start to the new year.

11:59 p.m.
Five . . . four . . . three . . . two . . . one . . .
Unhappy New Year! No sounds of cheering and merriment coming from downstairs, and still no word on what my punishment will be.
This is looking serious.

SUNDAY, JANUARY 1
8:00 a.m.

My new year's resolutions are to tidy my room more often, play computer games less often, and stop making enemies with supernatural beings. I was going to include learning Spanish, but I've had that one on my list for five years and I haven't done it yet, so I think I'll finally strike it off.

3:00 p.m.

I was called back into the study early this morning so Mum, Dad, and Grandpa could let me know my fate.

They said that we were in an unacceptable situation, with a pack of werewolves and a coven of vampires both living in the same small town. I thought Dad was about to formally declare war, but instead, he said we were all moving to Scotland!

317

He said that when they'd been in Edinburgh, they'd been invited to join a coven on the small Scottish island of Hirta. Dad said that he'd been tempted, but it would have meant registering with the Vampire Council again, and he was fifty years behind with his Vampire Council taxes. However, in light of the current situation, he'd pay his bill and take the Scottish vampires up on their offer.

I'm not sure how I feel about joining a larger coven, but I suppose things could have been a lot worse. Moving is stressful, but it doesn't really compare to battling your ex-girlfriend to the death.

My sister threw a fit when she found out that she was going to have to move again. She does it every time, so nobody took the least bit of notice.

She begged Mum and Dad to leave her here

with her friends, although she clearly hadn't thought it through. Does she want to stay ten years old while her friends grow up? I'm sure they'll still be fascinated with her talk of pop idols and magical unicorns when they're married with kids of their own.

MONDAY, JANUARY 2
1:00 p.m.

We've hired three large trucks for our journey to Scotland on Wednesday. Dad, Mum, and Grandpa will drive one each, and I notice that Mum and Dad are packing their stuff in their own trucks, as they don't trust Grandpa's driving.

I was annoyed that I'd been allocated only one third of the space in Grandpa's truck for my possessions, but I'm not sure I really care. Let him destroy my things, I'm not a materialistic person.

All I need is my diary, a pen, a PlayStation, an Xbox, a Wii, a laptop, a decent-size HD TV, surround-sound speakers, an iPod, an iPad, and a decent phone, and I'm happy. I wouldn't mind getting one of those chairs that vibrate as you play games, now that I think of it.

Needless to say, my sister moaned that she couldn't fit all her garish possessions in the truck. It's fine—I'm sure they sell worthless junk in Scotland too.

5:00 p.m.
Dad told me to pack all Grandpa's suitcases into the truck this afternoon, as he wasn't feeling up to doing it himself, surprise surprise.

Instead of thanking me, the ungrateful old fogy barked instructions into my ear the whole time. And to make things worse, he ranted on about how it was humiliating to move rather than battle the werewolves. He said that truces between werewolves and vampires were just supernatural correctness gone mad, and he wanted nothing more than a good old-fashioned scrap. I asked him if he was planning to join in with this battle personally or stand back and let everyone else do the work, as usual.

He got really angry and said that protecting the identity of werewolves was a very serious crime, and if he had his way, I'd be excluded from vampire society forever. And then he went right back to telling me how to pack his stuff! I couldn't believe his nerve. In one breath he was arguing that I should be expelled from vampire-dom for something I've already apologized about, and in the next he was ordering me about.

I couldn't take any more, so I smashed one of

his suitcases on the floor. It split open, sending ancient parchment and books flying in all directions. He started swearing and kicking me, and I realized it wasn't a good time to get in further trouble with Mum and Dad, so I set about picking it all up. But as I was doing so, I noticed something strange. One of the documents was a letter summoning him to court for failing to pay gambling debts—and it was dated 1752, more than a century before he claimed Dad transformed him.

As I rifled through the rest of his papers, more peculiarities emerged. There was the deed to a house on London's Fleet Street, which was dated 1706. There was a first edition of *Robinson Crusoe* inscribed for him by Daniel Defoe. And most incriminating of all, there was a late-eighteenth-century engraving depicting someone who looked exactly like him brawling inside a tavern.

I held out the engraving and asked if he'd like me to show it to Dad. Just like that time I told him I knew he had vampire strength, the anger drained from his face and he switched into false chumminess. He said that what my dad didn't know wouldn't hurt him and that some things should stay between friends.

I was tempted to present the evidence right away and demand the freeloading old buffoon be excluded from our coven, but I didn't have the heart. After all, it was one of my new year's resolutions not to make any more enemies. I said I'd keep his secret on the conditions that he didn't drink any more of my blood supplies, that I didn't have to do any more chores for him starting immediately, and that I didn't have to call him "Grandpa" anymore, but my sister still did. He agreed, and I left him to pack the rest of his cases into the truck.

11:00 p.m.

My sister has got over her tantrums about moving and now seems to be looking forward to it. Life must be so easy when you're shallow.

She wants to use the opportunity to change her name from Mavis. My parents promised she could do this when we moved, so they can hardly go back on it now. At first she wanted to be called something like Duchess Zaleska, Empress Kasadeja, or High Priestess Ysandrov, but Dad explained that vampires don't use these kinds of names anymore and that she'd only want to change it again as soon as we got to Hirta. In the end they agreed on Daisy, which is apparently popular again, though it doesn't sound much more modern than Mavis to me. She's chosen Isabella as a middle name, so her full name is now Daisy Isabella Mullet. She hasn't realized that her initials spell the word "dim," and I'm certainly not going to point it out just yet. I'm going to wait until she's told everyone her name and then write "DIM" all over her stuff on the pretense of helping her label her possessions.

I briefly considered changing my name from Nigel to something more macho like Chuck or Brad, but I don't think I'll bother. If those Hirta vampires don't think Nigel is a cool name for an eternal prince of the night, I don't want to be friends with them. It's quite a good filter when you think about it.

TUESDAY, JANUARY 3

I wasn't supposed to tell anyone we were moving, but I didn't feel like I could leave without saying good-bye to Chloe after all we've been through.

We arranged to meet on our favorite bench in the graveyard, as it holds many fond memories for us. Except for that time she tried to claw me to death.

I told her we were moving to avoid a vampire-werewolf battle. She said she was pleased she didn't have to rip my parents' throats out, as they'd always been very pleasant to her.

I told her she could continue using our house on full moons, as I know Dad won't get round to selling it for ages. She thanked me but said she'd tell her parents everything before the next full moon, so they could restrain her in their own basement. Her parents are very understanding, so I expect they'll be fine with it.

She's a bit nervous about her next transformations because they're going to occur just before her business studies exam, but she's factored three nights of thinking about nothing but grisly murder into her study timetable. You just have to be disciplined and plan ahead, like when you've got two exams on the same day.

She said she was sorry about the time she tried to force me to turn her into a vampire. I was going to commiserate with her for missing out on top prize in the supernatural lottery, but I thought I'd better not go there.

Instead, I told her she had no reason to be sorry and promised that if I ever bumped into her during any apocalyptic showdown between vampires and werewolves, I'd do my best to spare her.

She said she'd try to do the same, although she couldn't promise she wouldn't get carried away if she were in wolf form.

I said I understood, and with that, we parted.

5:00 p.m.
I just asked Dad loads of questions about

what it will be like in Scotland, but he told me to be patient. He said it was a much larger coven than he'd ever lived in before, with well over a hundred vampires. He also said that they have a school just for vampires. Even the teachers are undead! I'll think twice before disrupting those lessons. I'll be more likely to end up in a duel than detention.

It'll be weird to be around vampires my own age for once. I hope they're sensitive and intelligent like me, not just a mindless bunch of ghouls who boast about how many humans they've attacked. I'd better pack some good books just in case.

WEDNESDAY, JANUARY 4

I am writing this from the passenger seat in Dad's truck. I can tell it's quite a struggle for him to drive slowly, but Mum has no sense of direction and Grandpa refuses to use GPS, so it's the only way our little convoy can stay together. Plus, I think it's easier for Dad to drive cautiously when he has millions of pounds' worth of antiques in the back.

I wanted to stop for a picnic in the Lake District, but Dad said we couldn't drink any blood until after dark, as we have to be extra careful not to arouse any suspicion on our way to Hirta. He's even wearing a flannel shirt instead of a cape, which really isn't his style at all.

I'm so glad I'm in a different truck from my sister. There's nothing worse than listening to her moaning about how thirsty she is every time she spots some roadkill.

As I write this, we've just passed Stockfield Moor and entered the highway. Good-bye, streets; good-bye, hills; and good-bye, Chloe. It was a shame our love couldn't last, but I'll never forget the time we spent together.

Good-bye, Stockfield; good-bye, England; and good-bye, wimpy Nigel. After more than a century the time has finally come for me to leave my pathetic self behind and become the vampire I've always wanted to be.

ABOUT THE AUTHOR

Tim Collins is originally from Manchester and now lives in London. He is the author of eleven books, including the award-winning Notes from a Totally Lame Vampire (published in the UK as Diary of a Wimpy Vampire), which was nominated for the Redbridge Book Award, the Worcestershire Teen Book Award, and the Northern Ireland Book Award, and won Manchester Fiction City.

Find out more about Tim at his website: timcollinsbooks.com.